The Benedictines

THE BENEDICTINES

a novel

RACHEL MAY

Tammy –
Thanks so much
for being here +
chatting – it's been
great getting to
talk / getting to
Rachel

BRADDOCK AVENUE BOOKS

UNCOMMON BOOKS · UNCOMMON READERS

Printed in the United States of America
10 9 8 7 6 5 4 3 2 1

FIRST EDITION, February 2016

ISBN 10: 0-692-53801-2
ISBN 13: 978-0-692-53801-2

Cover design by Karen Antonelli
Book design by Savannah Adams

Sections from The Rule of Saint Benedict copyright 1981 by Order of Saint Benedict. Published by Liturgical Press, Collegeville, Minnesota. Reprinted with permission.

Alleyway Books
an imprint of
Braddock Avenue Books
P.O. Box 502
Braddock, PA 15104

www.braddockavenuebooks.com

Distributed by Small Press Distribution

The Benedictines

1

Windy pine-tree coast buttressed by smooth gray rocks. An ocean of white caps. Up the hill, a wide sloping green lawn, a driveway cutting through the center, winding between buildings. Students walk across the lawn, scarves and hair and jacket corners catching at the air. This is a place run by monks. Benedictines. There are rules to follow. Faith in God, Perseverance, Respect for Authority, Personal Accountability. *The incantation, heard again and again: myth of what we are.*

Bicycle

Brother Timothy is round on top with thin legs. He has a full head of hair. He used to be in business. Now he is a monk. His black robes go blowing in the wind when he rides his bike. It's a wonder they don't get caught in the spokes.

The teacher who lives down the road says his two dogs are scared of the monks. Says when the monks walk by in their robes, his two dogs bark at them. They must look like burglars, I say. All in black and walking slowly.

They are a mystery, even to the dogs.

Piper's Harbor is two hours north of Portland, Maine, and the lobster boats come and go and the barges with their tugboats slide slowly past the school all day. If you stand and watch, you wouldn't know if they're moving. Mark their place against the lighthouse on the far shore. Check back hours later, and see, oh, yes, they're inches past the lighthouse now.

Old oak trees line the drive at the top of the hill, and there is the yellow Victorian full of administrators, and a cluster of three-story brick dorms, Tudor-style, with peaks. At the back of the campus, there is the monastery, with a library full of old books. People say the collection is priceless. Whitman's handwritten edits. Emerson's letters to Louisa May Alcott. Things they hide away. Women are allowed there now, a rule changed ten years back. They cannot tour the Abbey, though. Only men may go there.

There's a stable for the students to ride their horses, and fifteen minutes up the harbor, a yacht club, rented out by the monks and frequented by the rich, sometimes by celebrities on hideaway vacations. Presidents. Former Presidents. Movie stars. Who will find them up here?

No one.

I teach here. I am a teacher, a woman, and only here for two years. *Visiting Artist* is my title, a position created by an artist alumnus.

Brother Timothy heads for the monastery. His hair is wet, stuck in black strands to his forehead. I walk inside, pull off my hood, and walk up three flights. We sit in the top floor of the art building, which is brick, and in the Tudor-style like the dorms. The students come in glum and full of complaints, shedding raincoats, feet in colorful rubber boots painted with ladybugs and turtles.

Write about something that ticks you off, I say.

We have two wide windows that look out to the whitecap sea. It is too warm for November. The sea frets, all unsettled.

Kathryn says, *Fuck global warming. Fuck it up the ass.*

Kathryn, I say. She is the rebellious one, who pushes and pushes.

The class laughs.

Margaret says, No kidding, this rain makes my hair so frizzy. It's so annoying.

Iris says, Have you seen *An Inconvenient Truth*? We're going to show it next week.

I'd never watch that movie, says Kathryn. What can I do about global warming? I want to keep driving my Lexus.

You can drive it less often, Iris says. Or get a hybrid.

Kathryn's turn and she writes that she wishes pot were legal, and that she had a better memory.

She says something to Ben about a spliff, and I say, Kathryn, okay, enough pot talk.

She says, How do you know what a spliff is? You smoke pot?

Pot is bad for your brain, I say. It turns it to mush.

Then Ben writes about sex, and how Catholicism makes you feel so guilty about it. How they shouldn't be made to feel bad.

I want to agree with him, but I cannot.

Margaret says, Did you know you can get Gonorrhea of the throat? I say this because I'm comfortable with you, Ms. James.

Well, thank you Margaret, I say, That's disgusting.

The class is roaring now: Gross! Foul! How does *that* happen?

Abigail makes the blow-job motion, rounded hand to mouth.

I wonder if there's a full-body condom, says Iris. You know, it could cover your whole body.

What would be the point of *that*? says Kathryn.

Everyone is laughing.

Well, you can get Gonorrhea of the throat. It's true.

Yeah, and you can get herpes of the eye, too, I say.

This was a mistake. I know it as soon as it comes out of my mouth. It was supposed to shock them into silence, but the class is going wild, everyone talking at once and laughing, laughing and saying how disgusting that is, and how does that happen? How do you get it *in your eye*? I look out the rain-splattered window to the harbor, where the sailboats rock on their moorings. If I walked outside, I'd hear the metal clips clanking against the masts, that comforting sound.

Round and round we go.

You're as red as your shirt, Ms. James! Look! Ruth points. Ruth is younger, a sophomore, and blushes when the talk turns this way.

We won't tell anyone, don't worry, says Abigail.

The point *is*, I say: Abstinence! Abstinence!

Abigail says, Well, I don't think I'm going to hell. I don't think God hates me.

No, I say, I'm sure you're going to Heaven. I'm sure God loves you.

They are all laughing, and just before they walk out the door, Kathryn holds up a giant penciled picture of an eye, and underneath it says: *Ms. James says you can get Herpes of the Eye*, in big block letters.

I imagine the monks walking in here today. Somber black robes. Talking of spirituality. Living abstinent lives of prayer and reflection. Imagine one of the priests. Imagine someone finding this piece of paper, with my name on it. With herpes written on it. Imagine myself sitting in Mr. O'Malley's office in the top corner of the yellow Victorian, explaining. *I thought it would shut them up*, I would say. *The lesson was to abstain! I told them they are too young for sex. And herpes of the eye is not an STD. It's the other kind of virus.*

Explanations he would not understand. He would stare at me, with his gray handlebar mustache twirled into spirals at each end, just the way he did at the beginning of the year, when I went into his office and asked if there would be any more surprise rules like the one I'd just learned. No, he'd said, that's it. It's a Catholic school. We can't very well have our single faculty inviting guests of the opposite sex to stay over. What kind of message would that send? I said, Even in my house at the edge of campus? Yes, he said. But I could have my brother over? I said then. Yes, he said, your brother. If in fact you have a brother. Just one, I said.

*   *   *

"The Rule of Saint Benedict, Chapter 1: The Kinds of Monks

There are clearly four kinds of monks. First, there are the cenobites, that is to say, those who belong to a monastery, where they serve under a rule and an abbot. Second, there are the anchorites or hermits, who have come through the test of living in a monastery for a long time, and have passed beyond the first fervor of monastic life. Thanks to the help and guidance of many, they are now trained to fight against the devil. They have built up their strength and go from the battle line in the ranks of their brothers to the single combat of the desert. Self-reliant now, without the support of another, they are ready with God's help to grapple single-handed with the vices of body and mind" (Fry 20).

4

*　　　*　　　*

Every week: CCD and church. The Ten Commandments, the Saints, the Gospels, the Books of the Bible. Color in pictures of Jesus. Sing songs. Listen. Quietly. Learn: No craving things you cannot have. No lies. No greed. No sex. If you do certain things, you can confess and be forgiven. If you do certain other things, you go straight to hell. Venial versus Mortal. There is Purgatory, which you can wait your way out of. People used to be able to pay your soul out after you died. Not anymore. You only get to Heaven if you're very, very Good.

Priests were men. Altar boys were boys. Women could give communion. And have babies. Their job in the church was: mothers, prayers, servers of the poor. Be a nun!

*　　　*　　　*

Brother Timothy

Stands in the middle of the dorm hallway at midnight, wearing a bright orange hunting jacket over his vestments. Hands splayed wide, fingers open. Shouting: "I'm a fire! I'm a fire!"

Brother Timothy is the Fire Marshall. He says everyone must be vigilant. Must know the fire escapes. And take the attendance list with you, when you go. So that you know who is missing. Leave a copy by the door. Walk quickly. Stay calm.

His robe drapes over his round belly. He likes fat sandwiches. He likes beer.

He has jowls for cheeks and red-bloodshot-eyes.

He says: *So, tell me about your dog.*

He says it smiling, lips pursed, waiting for a story. I don't have a story. Am not good at this, spitting out my life on command.

Some people are. Some people love to talk.

She is small and yellow and very sweet, I say. He nods and turns away. Not interested.

One of the students said, the other day: My mother told Brother Timothy the buildings were ugly and she wanted to spray-paint them gray.

Brother Timothy, she said, still isn't over it.

Brother Timothy has two sons. They are thirty and thirty-two. All the monks have had wives. Families. Then, when they are finished and old and feeling a little bit lost, they come here. To *Saint Christopher's*. (Say it with respect in your voice, please.)

The students say, We hate it here. All these rules. No hand-holding. No respect for our lives. We don't even learn anything I haven't learned a thing and Mrs. Brantz said, We've all been seeing too much of your backside, Abigail. And all the teachers gossip about us, they do, they do. We know they do.

Fuck Fuck Fuck Fuck Fuck, they say. They want to swear and swear and swear. The only way they have of saying: We are every kind of tied up around here.

I could tell them so many things, but I have to stay quiet because it is not my place. I am a teacher. They are the students. I have to say: Yes, yes, but: The rules have their purpose, no?

NO!

I agree with them, on most fronts. What I could have said to Brother Timothy: *I am from Colorado. I have a brother and two sisters. I am not a Catholic anymore. I think this place is haunted.*

One boy wishes for a Jack Daniels river to run through campus, and by accident, I say, Yes, that sounds nice.

When someone writes about Vermont in the first line and then transitions to a one-page story on Bermuda, I say: Yes, Vermont is lovely, isn't it?

The students laugh. The students say: He wrote about *Bermuda*, Ms. James.

Ah, I say. I know. I laugh.

I am thinking of my collage, the little red pieces that make the dancing woman's shoes. I am thinking of Crested Butte, where the mountains rise up high and snowy. No snow here yet. It is hot today, sixty-five in November. It is Springtime weather, and always blustery. This wind! My God! Will it never stop!

My Devout Roommate comes home and sits down on the couch. She is five-foot-two and calls herself *the bullet*, a nickname from her soccer days. She has such blonde hair and such fair skin that she has no eyebrows and has to put on sunscreen every morning, all over her body. Walks to school in her khakis and blazers smelling of coconut. We live a mile from campus, on its furthest edge, in a little cove near two other faculty houses, all clustered together at the end of a dirt driveway. We share this house, rent-free, as it's owned by the school. Our windows face the sea on one side, the piney woods on the other. This is her first year teaching, fresh out of undergrad; she didn't even have to take any master's courses, because this is a private school. She'll get the teaching degree along the way.

I want to tell her to go and get a life. I suggest a hobby. Card-making? Collages? Would you like to learn how to knit? I could teach you.

My Devout Roommate laughs and says, No thanks. She turns on the TV. Watches that nun who talks about art. Snacks on Swedish fish. There's a pile of papers stacked up beside her, waiting to be graded.

My Devout Roommate ignores me on campus. Doesn't want to be associated with This Sinner.

I flip through the school newspaper she left on the table, see the announcement about the memorial. I say how I would love to go to the Pet Memorial. A candlelight ceremony for those pets we've lost! Wouldn't that be fascinating? And my roommate says, So you can laugh at them? That's so mean.

No, I say, not to laugh at them. Just to see what a pet memorial would look like.

I call my brother that night. He lives in Utah. He says there's so much snow he'll have to call in sick tomorrow and go to Bluebird, a ski day. I tell him I should have married Danny, shouldn't have run away like I did—and all this way, too, all the way to Maine. It's too far away. I don't understand this landscape, I say. Always, the wind. And the ocean with its whitecaps. And the teachers with their buttoned-up shirts and their blazers, their attendance at church, their shiny loafers.

I don't fit here, I say.

He says, Danny was no good for you. It's good you left.

Yeah, I say, yeah. I tell him no one likes me here, and he says, Well of course they don't. You're a huge sinning slut.

I laugh, surprised. I keep on laughing and laughing and laughing.

*   *   *

The legend goes: Campus is haunted by a man who was an English teacher here, who killed himself one night in his classroom. He carved an A into his chest before he died, and some say it's because he was having an affair with one of the teacher's husbands, and some say it's for Saint Anthony, the Patron Saint of Lost Souls. He wanders the halls at night, and sleeps by day in the old English classroom in which he taught, Room 220, and that is why sometimes the books will fall off the shelf even when the windows are closed, when no one is moving. If you walk through campus alone at night, sometimes you can see him floating about, and the A on his chest will glimmer in the moonlight. Mr. Souci found him. They say. That's why he had the heart attack two years later. All that stress.

*   *   *

Talking Man

He is the sort of man who dodges you with words. The way he strings them all together without a breath until you want to say: *but!* Red in the face.

But you do not. You listen and you smile because you are a little too polite. Later, you will learn. He has the accent of a Boston man, the flat narrow eyes of a Mormon, yellow-flecked brown. His smile is tight and strained, browned teeth.

Now that you are surrounded by brothers and priests, you begin to wonder who these people are. You would like to make a survey for the monks as if in *Glamour* magazine: Your black gown represents: a) your simplicity as a monk b) your attempt to look clerical—no, *clergical*. c) your secret desire to cross-dress.

Well?

The Catholic Church has some problems. Not your fault.

So this man keeps on talking, and he says, *Why don't we get some coffee sometime?* And this sounds rather like a date. This particular man is quite a Catholic himself. Nearly a priest. Sometimes, when he talks about his Seminary Days, you imagine him in his swimming trunks with a little black collar. In his sweatpants at the gym with a little black collar. Teaching college students in a little black collar. That little prudish square of white (contain! contain!). He talks about how much he wants a partner in life, how the priesthood would not give him that. God was not enough. Just say it. God was not enough.

Now he justifies his almost-sex-acts. The women he has loved.

He lists them for you. Lisa, Jennifer, Kathryn, Amelia. Think of the children's book. She dressed the turkey in baby clothes. She never heard things right. He tried to abstain because that's what God says is right. But he is thirty-three and time slides on and he is feeling all alone. He says, I regret the end of that relationship because we were perfect for each other. And you say, How's that? Where is she now? And he says she was needy. Says she is married.

Another story goes: There once was a priest here who left the priesthood for another man's wife. He was best friends with that other man, and now the other man is a mime of his former self. Walks around listless. Or bitter. Trying to make jokes but the laughter never hitting his eyes.

Another priest was sent away for a while, to Boise (or Sante Fe?). Just recently, he came back. Eats all alone in one corner of the cafeteria. Rarely says hello. Which makes you wonder. There's no shrugging off the headlines.

There's a smell of church here—stale. Unleavened bread and incense combined. How it settles down upon the wooden seats, the green Victorian couch in the office building, the science teacher in his little red bow-tie set perfectly on his narrow neck. All these overblown families here, eating up the food, pushing out against the world.

Talking Man says, —and my father has a lazy eye and my mother's wicked German accent. Catholic Germans. They survived the Holocaust, he says, my grandparents. He says, I have so much history.

Makes jokes of being gay, how he loves fashion.

But it is Maine! The smallness of it and your isolation and your long walks through that goddamned *meadow* every day, from where—the view, my God! To kill for as they say: tall grass sloping down to blue blue bay, little sailboats tilted merry in the wind, and across the way, a white New England light house, and up the bay, that old white mansion whose windows glint when the sun goes down—but it leads nowhere, that meadow—only to the dormitories and the offices and the people closed up in their little Catholic world.

Talking Man says, We are getting old now. It is time to start thinking. Babies, you know.

The procreators of the world.

Talking Man says, Some girls want a daddy.

You roll your eyes.

One night, home alone in the house at the edge of campus, you plant little bulbous plants into pink pots, pack them in with fresh moist soil. Nurture what you can. Line them up in the windowsill in rows.

Talking Man says, I know so many women whose hearts have gone cold. Soulless. They seem to have souls at first, and then— no. They only want sex.

You say, Stop talking.

Say, Be a little braver with your heart.

Say, Let go all those rules.

And here's the miracle: he does.

The monks shed their robes. Walk the campus naked. Now we know what's underneath. (Is that why you have the robes, to take away imagining?) You cannot take away lust, Talking Man. It is there beneath your skin and it will skim out through your pores if it must. It will make itself known. You cannot talk it away.

And here is where you: Let loose. Open up your mouth and let the black crows fly out in threes. Cawing in their loud and crooked way. Nothing beautiful in it but the flight.

*   *   *

"...Third, there are the sarabaites, the most detestable kind of monks, who with no experience to guide them, no rule to try them 'as gold is tried in a furnace' (Prov 27:21), have a character as soft as lead...Fourth, and finally, there are the monks called gyrovagues, who spend their entire lives drifting from region to region, staying as guests for three or four days in different monasteries. Always on the move, they never settle down, and are slaves to their own wills and gross appetites. In every way they are worse than sarabaites. It is better to keep silent than to speak of all these and their disgraceful way of life. Let us pass them by, then, and with the help of the Lord, proceed to draw up a plan for the strong kind, the cenobites" (Fry 21).*

*   *   *

Brother Matthew in the Faculty Meeting

He's a fat boy! he says. That's the thing we're all not saying. A fat boy! Same as his father. I told his father as much at the conferences this year. Said, He looks like you probably did twenty years ago! He's fat! He can't draw because he can't tell how much pressure he's putting on the pencil because he's so fat! He is grossly obese, and it's just a fact.

Laughing, laughing in the back row. The teacher beside me, Talking Man, draws a cartoon. Big bubble eyes. Bulging. He draws in little veins, zig-zagging through the whites of the eyeballs.

Brother Matthew has snow-white hair and rosy round cheeks. Brother Matthew is tall, with muscles. He is very fit. He is rather a fox of an old man.

If Brother Matthew proposed a night of sin, who would I be to refuse?

I am only kidding. Half.

Next on the list of failing students is a boy who seems awfully nervous. Won't look you in the eye. His hand shakes every time he reaches for a cupcake, a cookie, a piece of paper from the center of the table.

What to do?

No one proposes the school psychiatrist. They say, Give it time. Wait and see.

Next comes a student who used to love sports and now only loves his girlfriend. Got some piercings this summer. Has really changed. Brother Matthew says, Something happened this summer, and if you can figure out what it is, that's the key here.

They propose the psychiatrist.

Maybe the boy simply fell in love. Maybe he is only becoming a teenager. A real live teenager. Like Pinocchio.

They are all so tired of these walls. The rules.

In the beginning of the year, when they said: No overnight guests of the opposite sex, I walked up to my boss's office, sat down and said, We need to talk about this, please. He said, It is the rule.

Can my brother come to visit?

Yes, he said. Family is okay. He twirled his handlebar mustache with one hand and rested the other on his belly. He has ten children. Three in college, seven stretched across elementary and high school. His wife is very very tall with short gray hair. So thin that when she stands in the wind, she bends.

Okay, I said.

But we don't want to find out at the end of the year that you only have one brother when you introduced us to five of them in the year.

A ha ha ha. I laughed. Wouldn't that be funny. No, no, I only have the one.

Later, on the phone, my mother said, Why'd you tell him that? You should have said you have at least three!

Ma!

Even my mother knows. The nature of these rules. She is not like she used to be, when we were young. Not so rigid about all this.

The Abbott broke the rules himself, slept with someone else's wife.

Now we sit around and talk about the students' problems. No one here would like to discuss their own issues, I see. Obesity. Latent homosexuality. Anger.

I am thirty, I said to the boss. Come on. Well, he said, Then you'll have to go to his house.

Not like they don't know. They know. Just put on a good show, that's what they want. Just make it look like you're not doing anything wrong.

The patriarchy. The play.

What can you do. There is nothing you can do. You are broke. You need this time to paint. Money from the devil. Keep your head down. Take good notes. Tell the students as much good as you can. Then leave.

*   *   *

Some people say that Mr. Souci found him because he was on his way to see him that night. Some people say that Mr. Souci's heart attack was not from stress but from a broken heart.

Mrs. Souci has two daughters. Mrs. Souci is one of the kind ones here. It would be nice to talk about these things, to talk about the truth behind these stories, her sadness. But this is a story that cannot be spoken. Like so many stories here.

*   *   *

Dear Ms. James, Re: Your Grades,

An email from the balding tall thin blockhead—blonde poofs above each ear—in the Admin Building, which always smells of must and incense. The Victorian at the end of the driveway. To the right, the bay, a wide green Gatsby lawn sloping to the water.

Happy Spring! says the email. *As the term begins, please try to keep your grade median to a 70. It was too high last term. Thanks, Blockhead.*

Why won't he ever call me by my first name? Which is Anne. This place.

Last night, I had a date with a man with no ass. Who loves his dogs too deeply. Baby-talks to them. Wears his cell phone and his Blackberry on his belt. Things I've learned about him this week. We met while walking our dogs at the beach. I thought that was romantic, boded well. Nope.

Do you want to drive my Beamer? he said on the date.

I don't care about cars, I said.

It's fun to drive, he said. Just try.

And he pulled over and got out, and I said, Oh, all right, why not?

And I felt, when I pressed the gas, the quickness of it, the fast slip up, faster, how it was ready. And I pressed the gas down harder, and the car jerked forward. Faster, faster, I drove that car as fast as it would go, down the highway, and he was right. It felt good. The way it picked up fast. The way it held the curves. For a minute, I was high on it. I laughed. Hands on the wheel and the way we just went. As if we could anywhere. And all those pine trees, and all that land, and all the other people—they did not matter. We were flying past them.

I slowed down, and looked at him. He held the bar on the door. He was afraid.

It's all right, I said. I'm done now.

We switched places again, at a rest stop on Route 93, and he drove me home, a kiss on the cheek. Goodnight, I said. Thank you. I like your new Beamer after all.

Do you want to go out again? he said.

Oh, I said, Sure.

But I did not mean it. I got out of the car and the air was quiet, just crickets and the waves lapping and the light on the stoop was still on.

I waved goodbye as I went in, and closed the door shut behind me. Slipped out of my shoes so I would not wake My Devout Roommate. But heard her on the phone in her room, giggling, saying, *Yeah, yeah, I know!* I crept upstairs and read a new book in bed.

I could hear the sound of the waves as I fell asleep, the light still on. I let the book fall against my chest, and as I drifted off, I thought I heard footsteps (soft, shoeless) down the stairs, a pause and shuffle for shoes, and the sound of the front door closing.

A very soft *click*, not its usual thump—the sounds of someone sneaking away.

But it was one of those things you can't be sure of, half into dreaming already.

*   *   *

First confession: When the priest asked if I'd committed any sins, I said: teased my sister and lied to my parents. Anything else? he said. No, I said, nothing. But. I'd stolen a poster from the book club. First grade. The posters were on the table at recess, and no one was there, and I hadn't bought enough books to get a free one. There were extras, though, of two golden retriever puppies. I wanted it so badly that I took it off the table and refolded it and stashed it away. Later, my brother came into my bedroom and asked why I'd thrown the poster in the trash all crumpled up. Why'd you do that? he said, That was stupid. Leave me alone, I said. Leave her alone, said my mother.

First communion: A white dress with polka dots pressed into it. I loved the texture against my fingers. A white veil, too, and a white cardigan sweater because it was still cool out, and best of all, a white veil. Stood in front of the fireplace for a picture. Smiled.

*   *   *

Friend

I could sleep with My One Friend. He is so tall and thin, not my type—even though I like him very much—but I could sleep with him, I could.

Fuck.

I say to My Devout Roommate, What Talking Man needs is a good hard fuck.

That's crass, she says. I don't believe in premarital sex.

No? I say.

No, she says.

She's scrolling through Facebook; she's friended her students. There's another pile of papers beside her, waiting for the ticks of her red pen.

I've never met anyone like you, I say. Not in a very long time, at least.

You quit going to church, she says. But maybe it's time you started again.

Don't use our house to proselytize, I say. Please.

I'm freezing, she says, We need to turn up the heat.

And she cranks it up again, to eighty, and sits there in her tank top and her shorts, basking, smelling of coconut.

It's a little warm, I say.

We don't have to pay for it, she says, what are you complaining about?

I need cooler air so I can paint. I get too hot moving around when it's eighty in here.

She rolls her eyes. Artists are so *crazy*, she says.

I go to the wall and turn it down to seventy, then walk into the kitchen to make hot chocolate. Sometimes, I imagine crumpling this whole campus up into a tiny little ball, and tossing it into the air, and casting it into the sea. I imagine how it will swirl and sink slowly—the church, the yellow Victorian, the Arts building, the Admin building, the wide green soccer fields, the great sloping Gatsby lawn—all of it swirling into the dark dark depths, where it will settle on the floor, and leave me, rescued and standing on the rocky shore.

I pull the cocoa tin from the cabinet and take a mug from the dish rack. Open the tin and spoon out the cocoa. Three scoops. Rich.

From the living room, My Devout Roommate says, Annie?

Here it comes, I think, another bout. I sigh. Yes, I say.

There is a pause. Then: Do you ever feel like there's something about yourself that you don't know?

I hold the spoon mid-air, about to dip into the cocoa.

What? I say.

I was expecting more of the heat talk.

You know, she says, Like maybe there's something else about you?

I look into the hot chocolate. I try to stall, wondering what she is telling me. Uh, I say.

Well—no, I say. Why?

No reason, she says.

Her voice is light, and I set down the spoon and go into the living room. She is on the couch, Andie curled up on the rug beside her. She is wearing her shorts and tank top, now reading one of her student's papers, making red checks and x's. She moves the pen in efficient, brisk ticks.

Are you okay? I say.

She doesn't look up. I'm fine, she says. She glances up. Says, Stop *hovering*.

And her voice is cold again, and I walk away.

*   *   *

At low-tide, there is a man outside, in the cold, in waders, up to his knees in water, poking at the sand with a pole. He is clamming, in this cold. Wears a red hat and fat brown mittens.

The seals are in the harbor, migrating north for the winter. See their Labrador heads pop up to the surface at dawn. See the sun come up over the horizon—a flat span of sea before the wind picks up. Smell the air, full of salt. Curled hair. Books pages that curl up overnight. Collage pages hanging in the spare room, curled over now. Nothing untouched by the damp.

Hear the sound of a boat hull rubbing against the dock, and think, before turning to see the boat and understanding what it is, that it's a whale song. Their high-pitched talk, the call that finds friendship, underneath the sea, across all those water miles.

*   *   *

Spasm

He walks down the street shaking his arms, quick little movements—sharp into the air and back to his body again. He crosses the street in a flurry, black robe dazzling up and down in the wind. When he gets to the other side, he shakes his head back and forth and his arms spasm, as if he disapproves of something.

I turn to look at him as I drive by, to see if he is talking. His lips are closed. His big black square glasses sit big and black and square upon his nose, which is crooked and bumped. His eyes set close together, and his hair a black tousle on the top of his head. If I want to laugh, I might call him Ernie. As in Bert.

He is a cartoon to me because he never says hello when he's out walking and passes me by. Only one time, just once, in December, he said, *Always wearing those sunglasses. Got to look cool.* The sun was at two o'clock and it hurt my eyes. I have sensitive eyes. People here notice everything—*everything*—you do. It is February. Snow falls every day, and the wind cuts up from the water.

In the dining hall yesterday, Valentine's, one of the teachers came in with her brood, all of them with their hair combed and parted and their shirts tucked into their jeans. They are a Tidy Family, led by Two Tidy Parents who have a penchant for camel hair. Big tan coats waltzing all over campus, topped with well-groomed dark narrow heads.

It was a snow day. She wore her pearls with her sweats. Pearls with sweats. She brushed back her daughter's hair and said, Happy Valentine's Day. I said, Oh I forgot it was. She laughed. Big white teeth. I just smiled, because I didn't know if her laugh was meant to be forgiving or self-satisfied. I wanted to say: Pearls and sweatpants is a little elitist, don't you think?

I think of Danny, the dream I had last night: I was back in Crested Butte. I kissed him over and over again. Tell myself: He was no good for me. Only wanted to be buoyed up. Said unkind things. Stop myself from picturing those snow-topped mountains, to imagine that dry air against my skin, or the sun reflecting off the snow on my favorite hike up Nomad Trail.

Before they got there, the dining hall was empty, and then one other teacher walked in, an older man who is kind and has a black-haired-English-teacher-wife and a sweet, curly-haired granddaughter who lives with them and is always very quiet. She is three or four. The last time I saw her, she wore a pink snowsuit and her arms were straight out beside her, and they could not settle against her body because she wore so many layers underneath. Her grandfather wrapped her scarf against her face. The wind blew. It was cold, in the teens. My dog ran around her in circles, and she lifted her hands straight up, and then put them down when my dog ran away.

In the dining hall, when it was quiet, he told me about his farm, and how he would build a log cabin, and fix up the barns, and get the kids a pony. Everyone loves a pony. I said: That's my dream, too, a farm. And he said, People around here, they don't know what they're missing. They're content here. But it's not really a home because when you retire, you have to leave. And in the meantime, you live in a dorm with the kids. Yeah, I said, yeah. I want them to have a home, he said. When I was a kid, I ran through the woods all day. They helped paint the barn this summer. They help in the garden. It's great.

It sounds great, I said.

You should buy some land soon, before the prices go through the roof, he said.

Yeah, but I don't have any money, I said.

Outside, the snow fell. There would be no school that day, and the snow would turn to rain, the surface an icy sheen by nightfall. All the faculty children would go sledding in the afternoon. We would walk by, my dog and I, and say hello. Walk through the playing fields to the golf course. Through the golf course to the bay, a long winding route. Watch out for coyotes, said the teachers, with that little dog. The sound of laughter. The sound of the sleds sliding down the hill.

At night, here, the wind blows heavy against the trees, against the house, up from the water of the bay and into our lives. A rushing roaring sound, always. As if the waves will come crashing upon us. The old trees creak, their branches straining. When the branches rub up against each other, they whine—or maybe they are singing: *ahhh-ah-ah-ahh*. Sometimes, you can hear the coyotes in the distance, howling to each other.

Each day, I walk into the wind in my hat and my sleeping-bag-of-a-jacket, and my mittens and my boots. Bundle up.

The dining hall was quiet. It was a place where, for a moment, I felt at home. And then the Camel Hair teacher came with her Camel Hair Brigade, and then the throngs arrived, all the students tumbling in for breakfast with their talk and scuffing shoes and jackets slung off in the hallway.

Months later, long after I'd given up saying hello to Brother Spasm (whose real name, I learned, was Brother Michael), Talking Man said, He is not allowed to talk to you. Because of the temptation.

What temptation?

The temptation of the female body. He can't talk to you. Won't look at you. That's how he avoids those thoughts.

So he won't say hello?

Right, says Talking Man. And then, for the first time, he is quiet. He smiles a little and nods. *Gross*, I say. *That's weird.* Just like my students, this talk I've learned. Talking Man just shrugs.

*   *   *

A unicorn in a tapestry that hangs in the lobby of a dorm, above the altar where they hold Mass twice a week; each monk has a dorm for weeknight Mass. Two of the dorms come together now, though, because one of the monks is going senile. Slips up and says peculiar things (one night: One should never trust the flesh—I should know. Yes! It's what he said. No one found this alarming). The unicorn is surrounded by men and dogs; it is being hunted. It sits with its legs curled underneath. The tapestry is brown, with orange curlique flowers and reeds and birds drawn along the edges. It is well faded. The unicorn is magical. Its horn can give you everlasting life. Something about the Trinity in the unicorn—what was it? I try to remember, but I can't. I know that if you kill the unicorn, it will save you. On the other side of the dorm room, there is a blow-up Frosty the Snowman, cheer for the holidays.

*   *   *

20

Online

Gail says try the internet, that's how Bess and Allen met, you know, just give it a try, no big deal, everyone does it now. No, I say, no no no. Too embarrassing, and what if someone saw, from here? No, no. But, she says, there's no one there for you, isolated up there, just give it a try. It's been months since Danny. It's time to date a little. Why not? Just think about it.

Okay, I say. I'll think about it. Sure.

She says, You're just placating me, aren't you?

Yes, I say. And we laugh, and she says again, Come home.

But I cannot. I signed a contract, I have no money, I have to stick it out.

Ditch

They are digging a ditch behind our house and have turned up slate. A big pile of pieces of black and gray slate. My Devout Roommate and I talk about it in the morning, over cereal. Watch the men in the small bulldozer. Eat our Cheerios.

Later in the afternoon, My Devout Roommate is gone. I am standing on the stoop while my little dog Andie sniffs the dirt, talking to my friend Gail back home. Gail says, Those people are crazy. It isn't you, it's them! She is emphatic. Thanks, I say. Then Mr. Griffiths comes by with his dog Gabe, and Gail and I say goodbye. I set the phone down on the stoop. Gabe bounds up to Andie, and they chase each other around the yard. Andie is so happy for a friend, for a friend, please to play!

Mr. Griffiths wears a trench coat and a hat. He is a man in his sixties. He lived here for thirty years, and then the school told My Devout Roommate and I to move in, and Mr. Griffiths moved up the bay, closer to the yacht club. Come winter, he said, I left storm windows, you know. Said, Oh, you don't want to put those up yourself. You get the school to do that for you. Those are plate glass. Mr. Griffiths is right. Mr. Griffiths is kind.

He looks at the pile of slate. A ditch to prevent the Spring flooding (*Inches of water!* Talking Man told us. *Up to your shins! I'd walk in and Mrs. Griffiths would say, Upstairs, upstairs, there's food for us upstairs! Away from the water. Away from the flood.*)

He looks at the pile of slate and touches his hat and says, I didn't know they were going to dig there. I wish I had known. I asked Mick about that. Asked him this summer. He said they were going the other way. This is uphill, so I figured they wouldn't dig down this way. Geez, I wish I'd known.

When he walks up and down the hill to the bay each day, he looks in the windows. Sees me sitting there watching TV. Sees me eating a peanut butter sandwich. Sees me wasting my time. Guilt. When he looks in, I wonder how it feels to see someone else living in your own house. To see someone else's furniture. Someone else's taste. Someone else's life. My green couch sitting PLUNK in the middle of the room. I wonder how it feels to look in and see thirty years erased like that. Or, thirty years of memory slicked thick and unerasable in the air around the house.

Oh, I say, They started just this week. I stand on the stoop, in my socks. He whirls around to me. Whirls back to the pile. The belt of his trench coat swings loose against his back as he turns. The pile of broken slate. The soil here full of it.

In the early fall, a group was down on the beach, chiseling at the slate that sits in layers along the shore, holding up the dirt, the roots, the trees, that jut like small cliffs out over the stony beach. They chiseled with their gloves, delirious on their search. What are you looking for? I asked. Fossils! said a gloved man. He chiseled with his son. Big smile on his skinny face. I didn't say anything back. What I wanted to say: You are ruining the land. Look how those trees are sliding into the water! Roots exposed. You are helping it fall into the sea. Look at what you're doing! For a treasure you can tote home?

I buried two dogs there, says Mr. Griffiths. Put down concrete slabs and everything. I had markers for them. And I asked Mick if he was going to dig there. Because I would have done something about it if I'd known. He said they were going to go the other way. I wish I'd known. I'm just—I buried two dogs there.

Our two living dogs circle the house, ears pressed back to the wind.

I'm sorry, I say. Oh, that's too bad.

It is, he says. It's really too bad.

He puts his hands on his hips. Touches his hat. Touches his cheek.

This man who left his house of thirty years. I see him longing for it. See his dog turn into the drive every time he passes by. See him say: No, Gabe. And Gabe veers back, stays on the road.

They walk this route every day, from the house to campus, a half mile away across the fields and through the woods that reach down to the water. A tradition they must have had—to walk to the rocky beach and back again. To walk right down to the bay just before sunset.

The sunsets here are hot and red and fill up the whole sky, pink and red horizon against the black line of trees. Crayola colors. Thick and waxy and rich.

I'm so sorry, I say. Can I do something? We could make a new marker?

Well, he says. Maybe I'll come back down. You might see me down here one day, doing that.

Okay, I say, come anytime.

I feel it is somehow my fault, even though I had no idea he was supposed to live here. I wish they had not upturned those trees. Ruined the burial ground for his dogs. They chop down trees on campus all the time, even the oldest trees, to make the view better, or build a new building. Even the monks do not stop this, but pat themselves on the back and say, *What good stewards of the land we are. We plant a new tree each time we cut one down.* But what is a new tree? A sapling? It would take thirty years or more, I want to tell them, before it will grow into what you just killed. Animals lived in those trees. And the harbor up the way, which the monks rent out, it dumps gasoline and chemicals into the sea. A slick profit. But I am only here two years and want to slip out of this uninvolved, unscathed. So I ask about recycling bins, and say nothing else.

Mr. Griffiths says, There were dogwoods, too. They could have saved the dogwoods. I took care of those trees for twenty years. They were beautiful. They just tore them out. Didn't even try to save them. And the rhododendron...

I know, I say. It was ten feet tall.

At least, he says. More like twelve.

He shakes his head, and turns to go, and he calls to Gabe, and Andie follows.

Here, Andie! I say. Come here!

She's right here, he says. She's just here.

He and Gabe walk away, onto the dirt road, behind the brick wall. To the right, there is an oak still in the yard, and then a row of bushes and then the bay. I turn back to Mr. Griffiths. He does not say goodbye or even turn back.

I call out, Goodnight, Mr. Griffiths.

Inside, door closed, I try not to look at him driving up the hill in his car, try to stop thinking about him, about his lost dogs, the lost trees and gardens. I try to become less indignant with this place. But I know there is no stopping it, the anger that grows here. Old things I thought were gone, upturned now. Jagged edges, and the designs these pieces hold—precious swirling indents of shells. The print of a Neolithic fish. Fossils we love to trace with our fingers (*can you believe this was here? Look at what I found.*) We cut and dig and take. A compulsion. To better a place. To shore up the flood, to save the house, to improve the view, to prune the plants, to expand. To take these pieces home, and slip them into our palms, and tote them like souvenirs, burning in our pockets.

*   *   *

"B. Dress Code:
It is expected that all students wear clothes in keeping with Sunday service dress, with no holes, patches, or runs, and with neat presentation: shirts ironed and tucked in, belts worn with pants, dresses and skirts of appropriate pattern and style.

1. All boys are expected to wear a blazer and dress shirt each day, with the exception of the early fall and late spring, when short sleeved collared shirts are permitted and blazers are not required. Early fall ends October 1, and late spring begins April 20. All girls are expected to wear pants with blazer or sweater, or a dress or skirt with long sleeves or blazer/sweater. Skirts must fall to within one inch of the knee.

2. Students must wear appropriate shoes to class. Flip-flops and Birkenstocks are not permitted. Heels above one and a half inches are not permitted. Leather-soled sandals are permitted only before October 1 and after April 20.

3. Students must always be in accordance with the dress code at Daily Mass.

4. Boarding students are expected to shower and change between athletic practices and dinner. Dinner dress should be in keeping with the daytime dress code.

5. Any student in violation of the dress code can expect to meet with the Dean and to lose social or athletic privileges, as deemed appropriate by the Dean (St. Christopher's Student Handbook).

*   *   *

What the body knows: *Our father who art in heaven, hallowed be thy name. Thy kingdom come, thy will be done, on earth as it is heaven. Give us this day our daily bread…*And this: *Hail Mary full of grace the Lord is with thee. Blessed art thou amongst women and blessed is the fruit of thy womb. Holy Mary, mother of God, pray for our sinners…*Each sin earns a certain prayer, recited a certain number of times. Confess and then kneel down in a pew and pray off the sins. Twenty Our Fathers and Ten Hail Mary's. Or thirty and five, or ten and ten. How do they decide?

Mass: Prayers for others, the readings from the books of John and Mark, then the Gospel (he says: The word of the Lord, we say: Amen), the sermon, sign of peace (shake hands), sit kneel stand, sit kneel stand, smell of incense, taste of Communion: flat, sticky in the mouth as you try to chew. Walk up in a row, hold cupped hands for it, take it with one hand and put it into the mouth, walk back to the pew, kneel, pray. Stare at the stained glass windows, made in the seventies. Square-bodied Jesus with a round halo behind his head. *Dear God, Thank you for _____, please take care of Mom and Dad and Ed and Aunt Grace and Aunt Lisa….* Silence in church. Hands folded. Do not fool around. If we are good, we get ice cream afterwards. Or brunch, sometimes. If we are bad, our parents are angry. Ed always made me laugh. We were often bad.

My One Friend

says, Last year, I broke my ankle while I was skiing and my first thought was, Thank fucking god I won't have to coach squash this year. Thank god.

And then he laughed.

He is very tall and very thin, and balding now. He is from Gloucester, Massachusetts and wears wire-rimmed glasses and has narrow lips. Puts one hand behind his neck when laughs. Has that Massachusetts accent: *Wheah ah you?* We sit on my green couch, in the living room. He drinks whiskey. I drink water. There is a fire in the fireplace, and the wind blows against the house. A cold day. He has become my friend this fall, my only friend in this place, who will sympathize when I say how this place holds people in too much, who will listen when I complain about My Devout Roommate and her all-too-audible before-dinner and mid-day prayers. He is not happy. I know that. And I know, also, that he would like something more, with me. Two weeks ago, when he came over at ten o'clock to drop off a book I'd lent him, he stood leaning against the doorway for awhile, making chitchat, pulling his gloves off and on, asking was I lonely here? My Devout Roommate was away. If you're scared, he said, I could stay.

I looked down at my feet. Oh, I said, I really need the time to paint, actually.

And he said, Oh, right, and then quickly left.

I hate this place, he says now. Oh my god, I can't wait to get outta here. I'm leaving at the end of the year. I'm moving to Detroit.

I say, Detroit?

And he says, Yeah, Detroit. I can have a newspaper job there. I'm going. It's good pay. Be near my brothers again. Fuck. Why not?

Sure, I say, sure.

He says, I was thinking of breaking my ankle again this year. I can't drive that bus all spring, that fucking bus with all those kids gabbing. Oh my god, he says. It makes me want to die.

He laughs. Where's your roommate?

I don't know, I say. Studying, I guess. She's been working late up at the dorms.

I never see her up there, he says. Takes another sip of whiskey. Says, I saw her with Jessica earlier. They were driving off in Jessica's car.

Oh, yeah? I say, You know, maybe you can tell them you don't want to do it.

Nah, he says, I have to. They won't pay me otherwise. Shit, he says. Let's have a drink tomorrow, and I say, Sure, but what I want to say is what Gail tells me now: Just leave this place, just leave. I see that he is spinning into something, that he will drink and drink because it is the only thing he sees, the only salve.

*   *   *

Chapter 6. Restraint of Speech
Let us follow the Prophet's counsel: I said, I have resolved to keep watch over my ways that I may never sin with my tongue. I have put a guard on my mouth. I was silent and was humbled, and I refrained even from good words (Ps 38[39]:2-3). *Here the Prophet indicates that there are times when good words are to be left unsaid out of esteem for silence. For all the more reason, then, should evil speech be curbed so that punishment for sin may be avoided. Indeed, so important is silence that permission to speak should seldom be granted even to mature disciples, no matter how good or holy or constructive their talk, because it is written:* In a flood of words you will not avoid sin (Prov 10:19); *and elsewhere,* The tongue holds the key to life and death (Prov 18:21). *Speaking and teaching are the master's task; the disciple is to be silent and listen.*

Therefore, any requests made to a superior should be made with all humility and respectful submission. We absolutely condemn in all places any vulgarity and gossip and talk leading to laughter, and we do not permit a disciple to engage in words of that kind" (Fry 31).

*   *   *

Confirmation: CCD in high school was at night, a round table with the young priest who was said to be "cool." I didn't like him. Something about him. We talked about the church. We debated sometimes. I argued, saw no place for women in this church. We were going to be confirmed soon. These talks were supposed to prepare us. We took saint's names. I wanted Francis but had to have a woman. Margaret. Learned later that it was my grandmother's Confirmation name, too, which the family took as a good sign.

There were eight or so others, kids who played soccer and came from money and had lived in that town for a very long time. We'd lived there just a few years. Three girls who were best friends—Bennie and Jacqueline and Dominique—and a boy who kept his hair very short, whose named was Randolph. One girl who was quiet came to school so drunk one day that our friends had to hold her up and walk her to class. She'd sipped fruit punch with vodka from a thermos all morning.

When I was in college, that priest left suddenly. My mother told me over the phone. No one knew why he left. Says he disagreed with the head priest, who had been there for three decades. The younger priest was more liberal. But there were rumors, too, that he was having an affair. With one of the college boys. These trips he took the students on, to Guatemala and Honduras and Mexico. Build churches. Build houses. Growth experiences. This one college boy went every summer three years running. The boy said he wanted to be a priest, too. A cool priest, like this priest. They shaved their heads together one year. So the rumors ran.

*   *   *

Inquisition

Ms. James, says Iris, are you and Mr. L dating?

We are in the top of the Arts Building. It is December, wind raw in Maine. The sea is choppy, frilled with wind. A sailboat rocks past. The pines down by the shore sway a little back and forth. We sit in a circle in chairs with desks attached. Steven taps his pencil.

Well? says Iris.

No, I say. I turn back to the class. We are just friends. (I do not tell them that he is My One Friend here.)

Men and women can be just friends, says Kathryn. She nods. Affirming.

Yes, I say.

We saw you watching a movie with him, says Kathryn.

We saw you walking through town with him, says Iris. At first she doesn't mention him, first she says she saw just *me*, but then she says *with Mr. L.* As if she was trying to protect me from the gossip, but once the cat was out of the bag, well—all bets are off.

I like Mr. L, says Abigail. He's really nice. He's so smart.

He taught me how to write, says Kathryn. He's such a good writer.

He's a really good teacher. I really like him.

If you *were* dating him, says Kathryn, I approve. I mean, just so you know.

I laugh. Thank you, Kathryn, I say. You're so wise today. Like my grandmother with all these lessons.

She smiles.

Okay, I say, handing out sheets of paper. Grab a piece of sketch paper. Time to work.

What are we drawing? says Iris.

It's a game, I say. I'm going to give each of you a word. I reel them off and point: *tomato, umbrella, Spain, duckling, engagement ring, math.*

Linda got *engagement ring.* She says, Can I make a drawing of you and Mr. L?

No, I say.

Do you grade your papers together? says Maria. She says it singsong, teasing.

Yes, I say. I am tired of their questions. I say: Naked.

They are shocked. They all laugh. Then I laugh.

I shouldn't have said that, I say. It was a joke to make you stop asking questions.

But they are laughing. They are out of control.

They are shocked. They all laugh. Then I laugh.

You'd better wear your goggles, says Iris.

What? I say.

Oh! says Kathryn. She leans toward Iris. Watch out for the Eye Gonorrhea! You'll need your eye lotion! Ha ha!

Oh my God, I say. I put my face into my hands. Everyone is laughing hard now, ha ha ha ha.

A grading-papers booty call! says Abigail.

What's that? says Steven. He is the only boy in class. He is a freshman, blonde, blushes easily. His neck is splotched red.

It's when you call someone up in the middle of the night to have sex, says Maria. She nods. Matter-of-fact. Check that off our to-do list.

Thank you, Maria, I say, for clarifying.

He should know! says Kathryn. Otherwise he'll miss his chance if he gets one and doesn't know what it is!

Ha ha ha ha ha. They all laugh.

Steven is often late for class. He clowns at being disorganized. When I come into the classroom, he is face-up on my desk, stretched out, saying, *Miss James, I'm so tired*. He snores. All of this is a cover, for his uncertainty. He is afraid of looking foolish, so he always plays the fool.

New assignment, I say. I pass out Post-its.

Ooooh, they say, Post-its! They laugh and stick them and unstick them to the table, on each other's arms. Abigail puts one on her forehead. Steven looks at her and giggles.

I say, The new assignment is to write down a character's name and two details about that person. Then pass the paper to the person across from you. Your job is to draw the person they've described.

Steven writes down his details, his character, and passes his Post-it to Iris.

Iris reads her character. Says: *Adam Smithhumanbrownhair took a walk one day...*

I laugh because I realize.

Steven, what were the details you wrote down? I say.

He's a human and he has brown hair.

And his name is Adam Smith?

Yes.

Oh, says, Iris, I thought it was all one name.

Everyone laughs. Iris is embarrassed.

It's okay, I say. No big deal. And then she begins to giggle, and then everyone else is laughing, and I laugh, too, having held it in all through the Mr. L conversation. Now, it all spills out. And once I start, I cannot stop. I laugh hard, the kind of laughter that takes over, like in church. Like in the hush of something serious, people weeping—and there you are, laughing.

*   *   *

Chapter 68. Assignment of Impossible Tasks to a Brother

A brother may be assigned a burdensome task or something he cannot undo. If so, he should, with complete gentleness and obedience, accept the order given him. Should he see, however, that the weight of the burden is altogether too much for his strength, then he should choose the appropriate moment and explain patiently to his superior the reasons why he cannot perform the task. This he ought to do without pride, obstinacy or refusal. If after the explanation the superior is still determined to hold his original order, then the junior must recognize that this is best for him. Trusting in God's help, he must in love obey" (Fry 92).

*   *   *

Sent: Nov. 18, 2004

Anne,

I know this is a strange place, but remember that it is only for a little while. In two years, you can leave. Lucky you.

And – it's almost Thanksgiving, a little break.
                                        -- Mary Beth Souci

*   *   *

Gyrovague

The monk who wanders too much, he is slight with blonde hair and a beard and a mustache and eyebrows to match. He is very smart, you see right away. Something about the face. The way he uses his hands when he talks, the words he chooses well. He is from a monastery in Maine. He joined two years ago. He wears a green wool sweater with a hole in the elbow. His eyes are blue, and he has this cunning smile that reels you in. You watch his dimples as he speaks. You watch his lips.

Some monks have Brooks Brothers shirts, he says.

Any gift I receive has to be approved by the monks, he says. *They decide if I can use it or not.*

And who approves the Brooks Brothers? you say.

He says, *That's a mystery.*

You are at dinner, a cheap Chinese restaurant, with all the young faculty. They knew the Gyrovague from when he taught at St. Christopher's two years ago, before he became a monk. They are all old friends.

He says: *My father hates that I'm a monk. He doesn't understand. My mother loves it.*

Says: *I think I'm just going to be a wanderer most of my life, and I'm okay with that.*

The monks say the wanderer is lost, is looking for something that cannot be found.

He wants to write and read and spend time thinking.

You want to say: You could do the same in grad school, but with the added bonus of sex. Your Devout Roommate doesn't believe in premarital sex. Some of the faculty do—they sneak in boyfriends and girlfriends, hide their cars at the fish shop a mile away. But not her. She is steadfast.

You look at him and think you might be kindreds. But there will be no time to tell because the table is wide and you are hard of hearing and when he says, *Where's that again?* You think he says, *Wheresanabin?* Some other language he thinks you might know. The woman to his right dies laughing when you say what you heard. The woman to his right is Your Devout Roommate, blonde and fair, prayerful but mocking. She laughs at the wrong things. Mostly at you. You are trying to think kind thoughts about her these days.

The Gyrovague says, *I drank absinthe with the Abbott a couple of weeks ago.* He laughs. He looks up, catches your eye, and you laugh with him.

Your Devout Roommate says: *Oh that stuff is awful for you. I had a terrible experience.*

She makes a sour face and shakes her head. She talks about Florida, Spring Break, how she tried it there with friends.

Really? says Jessica on the other side of the table. *You tried absinthe?* She looks impressed. She has brown baloney curls like a little girl's and wide brown eyes. My Devout Roommate looks at her and nods. Red flushes up her neck, in her cheeks. Her fair skin blushes easily.

Where did you get it? says the Gyrovague. *How did you find it in Florida?*

My Devout Rommate shrugs. Waves her fork in the air. *Oh,* she says, *I don't remember. One of my friends.* The blush gets deeper, redder, spreads to her forehead and her ears. She pushes her fork into her noodles and spins.

Jessica watches My Devout Roommate and then looks at the Gyrovague and says, upbeat, So, you *like* being a monk?

When you talked to your One Friend on campus before the Gyrovague arrived, he said: *I've offered to be his escape car when he wants to jump the wall. I think it'll be sometime this summer. I said I'd bring him liquor and a woman. He needs to get laid. That's his biggest problem right now.*

You wanted to say: Tell me about it.

You wanted to say: Stifle sexuality long enough and you get meanness or perverts. Haven't you heard the news?

You say, *You'll bring a sacrificial woman?*

He laughs. Says: *Yes.*

33

That's sick, you say.

Your One Friend is tall and thin. He is a little bit older than the Gyrovague, and balding. The Gyrovague cannot be more than twenty-three or four. He is very young. Too young to sign his life away to abstinence and prayer. You think: He knows this but has not admitted it to himself yet.

You think: I have so much to do. I want to finish my collage. It is hanging from clothespins in the spare room right now. Tiny one-inch clothespins in multi-colors. You walk between the rows of hanging papers, scenes spread across each one, you duck under one row to get to the next, and you wonder how you will ever put it together. How you will make it whole.

You look up and call across the table, *You should leave. Get out of there, just go!*

He looks up, startled. He smiles. Two dimples. You want to touch his hands. You want to kiss his lips. You imagine it, then, how they would feel against yours. You would slide your finger into that hole in his sweater, and touch his skin.

What if I did? he says. He is staring, staring at you.

And you are lifting, lifting up.

Everyone else at the table is arguing about what happened during the lacrosse game, the ref's call toward the end, something unfair happened. You and the Gyrovague can hear each other fine. Suddenly, there is no need to strain or shout. You are speaking into this silence.

We could run north, he says. *To the mountains. To Canada.* He smiles.

All right, you say. *Sure.* You smile, too. You cannot help it. The smile just comes.

I'd read to you at night, he says, *and you could show me your paintings, and we would live wherever we felt like living.*

And I'd knit us sweaters, you say.

And he laughs and says, *Yes*.

And there is this imaginary life in that moment: The way your lives could be, how you would run across the world together, how nothing from this place would matter, how you would live together the kind of life you dream. It could be like this.

He laughs. He stares at you a while, and the rest of the people go on talking and eating, oblivious.

You say: *Yes.* And you let this dream go on spinning, trying not to believe in it too much. But believing in it anyway, whole-heartedly. It feels reckless. It feels good.

*   *   *

*   *   *

Pawtucksey Independent
Monday, November 8, 2004
      Residents Pitch in for Piper's Harbor Clean-up
      Three Pawtucksey High School Students Go to National Science Fair

*   *   *

Dear Teachers,

he says, There will be no bells on Friday.

He is in charge of the bells. He of the bald head—blonde poofs—and the bobbing walk. He wears Converse All-Stars high

35

tops on his off days. They say he used to be in a Christian punk band. Sometimes he'll play air riffs when he walks through campus. Brought a pile of wood to our house so we could have a fire in the fireplace, in the morning, before we woke up. An act of generosity that gave me hope. Some people here, they have good hearts. They mean well.

Dear Teachers, Please come to the faculty meeting on Wednesday at eight a.m., when we will start with a prayer and proceed with a series of inanities. (We will wonder why you are not mouthing *The Our Father*, Ms. James, but will just look at you and look away, saying nothing.) You will waste your lives away in that vaulted lecture room where the chairs are bolted to the floor and swivel back and forth. You will watch the big clock behind our heads tick tick tick on slowly, and you will revert to your own high school days, passing the time by writing notes and making jokes and being altogether silly.

Everyone has an Agenda. The English Department thinks the library should function as a library rather than a social area. The Language People need more teachers; nineteen in a class is too many for recitations. The Science People want a better building, more up-to-date equipment. They have almost all the funds. Seven million dollars. Say it like the Sesame Street Count: *Seven million a ha ha ha ha!*

People go mad in this place.

Dear Ms. James, he wrote the day he dropped off the wood, The Wood Fairy made a visit to your house today. I hope you find it.

2

"The life of a monk ought to be a continuous Lent. Since few, however, have the strength for this, we urge the entire community during these days of Lent to keep its manner of life most pure and to wash away in this holy season the negligence of other times. This we can do in a fitting manner by refusing to indulge evil habits and by devoting ourselves to prayer with tears, to reading, to compunction of heart and self-denial" (Fry 71).

*   *   *

Walk

The monks walk all over campus, black robes breezing in the wind behind them. Black robes black wool hats black shoes. I wonder if they wear white underwear. Wonder if they have to put their whites in separate loads.

One of them wears white socks when he goes to the gym. Brother Spasm. The bearded skinny one. He carries a book and wears his black shorts, his black shirt, his black orthopedic shoes, his white socks, and he walks to the gym and works out.

Goes around the Holy Lawn, the green square in the middle of the buildings. The church on one side, the classroom buildings, the Admin building. *Don't walk on the Holy Lawn.* There's no religion to this. It is just tradition.

I walk my dog at ten o'clock at night. She is restless by then. She needs a stretch before sleeping. Down here by the bay, it is dark and all the trees creak in the wind. They are old trees—oaks and birches and maples and beeches. They have a row of knuckles up their trunks on the road-side, from where their branches were trimmed back. The branches on the yard side reach out and out, zagging against the blue sky.

Sometimes I am very scared walking alone at night. No one else walks down here. I look down to the water and hear the buoy rocking back and forth with its clanging bell. The water is dark. The moon shines on it. I half expect a man swimming in the bay. Horror film.

On this night, December, I walk up to campus and turn left, down the driveway. Walk past the little graveyard where every monk is buried. Walk past the house to the left that is all lit up with a family inside. And then, running from the dumpster comes the father from the lit-up house, and his two dogs, who run up to greet my dog. All their tails wagging. My dog's whole rear-end wags because she has no tail. The father says, *Are you going for a walk? Shall we join you?*

This is good. I have been working all alone all night. Paint all over my hands and arms. Hanging pieces up to dry on the clothesline. *Yes, please!*, I say.

So we go walking. Through the campus and into the fields where I am scared to go alone at night. Fields where the coyotes hunt. I have been warned. They will eat my little dog if they find her alone. Now, the dogs race together—except for his little one, who stays close to his heels because she does not like my dog— and we talk about Vermont. Thank God for the snow in Vermont. And we talk about how expensive lacrosse sticks are these days. One hundred and fifty dollars for a hockey stick! Unimaginable. And we talk about his wife's job medicating the sick. She is a nurse.

The father is kind, and he talks about teaching and he has a mother who lives now in the town where I grew up. His mother is declining. I don't know what it is like to have a mother in decline, but I imagine it is very sad. She only sometimes remembers things. She lost her license and does not understand why.

This must be a confusing way to live.

At the great white windmill, we look up and laugh because Brother Joseph has put a star up there, somehow. A white lit-up star as big as one of the smaller dogs. How did it get up there?

Amazing, we say. The father says the monks are a Cranberg nightmare, and I say what is Cranberg? and he says it's the company that regulates the use of machines. I laugh.

Then he goes his way, hands in his pockets, waving goodbye, and I go mine. I am alone again. My One Friend is away. The Gyrovague is gone. It is all right. My little yellow dog and I walk home, the sound of the buoy in the bay calling us back.

*   *   *

Dear Faculty,
There will be a special Mass on Tuesday for Father Delmoon, who passed away this weekend after a long internment at St. Jude's Special Care facility in Portland. The Mass will be at 8 a.m., and all students and faculty are required to attend.
> *Thank you.*
> *Headmaster Swift*

*   *   *

At the bay, the water freezes as it leaps onto the rocks, leaving long whitish drips over their tops and down their sides. As if the water is still moving. As if it got caught mid-air.

*   *   *

Tin Box

Brother Matthew keeps the money. He sits at a desk in the Administration Building, which is made of dark brown wood with arched ceilings inside, and he holds onto a little tin box, where all the students keep their money.

He has a beard. He wears big black square glasses. He is the thinnest of the monks, tall and lean. Flecks of brown in his gray beard, remnants of who he used to be.

He says hello and smiles. Leans down and pats my little yellow dog. He says, Would you like a treat? And the women behind him, both with their gray bobbed hair and their rosy cheeks and big bellies, they laugh and say, Oh so cute! Oh look at her! My little yellow dog lolls her pink tongue and gets three cookies.

The students walk in and say, Hi Ms. James! They wear khaki pants in funny colors: green and red and blue. They make the best of the dress code.

The *boys* have a dress code, says Mr. O'Malley.

This means the boys wear coats and ties and the girls wear whatever they like. Short skirts that they tug down with two hands, blouses open too wide. My Devout Roommate came home one day saying, *Did you see Janet McDonald's cleavage today? Oh my God, that shirt was way too low. But her breasts are amazing.* She said it as if she was repeating what someone else had said. Proud. Waiting for me to agree.

Back in class, Kathryn says, I hate Babette! I spent seventeen hours with her, I can call her Babette now!

She's Mrs. Dregville, I say, Please, some respect.

Ms. James, says Iris. Are you dating Mr. L now? You look really good.

Thanks, I say, No. Look, we can have some fun in here, but you can't curse out the teachers in front of me.

Yeah, says Kathryn, you do look good. She turns to the others in the circle. Says, Fuck Mrs. Plume. I got a D on my test and now I'm in study hall every afternoon!

She waltzes in late because of her clarinet lesson, three times in a week, hands me a note with a smile. Not *my* fault, she says.

She is getting more and more rebellious, because I have not drawn the line, have not been able to stop her, do not want to be the bad guy on a campus full of rule-enforcers. But I am getting fed up.

What we need here is some R-E-S-P-E-C-T, I say. Some for me and some for each other. Get it together, people. Please. No swearing or you're headed for Mr. O'Malley's office.

They do not listen. Spring Vacation is coming at the beginning of April. They are wild on hope. Two long weeks—no, almost *three*, they say, like a very small child clarifying his age. Five and a *half*.

Yes, I say, Almost three.

I am looking forward, too. I am looking forward.

Now the flowers bloom—tulips and daffodils and chrysanthemum. But in Crested Butte, my brother said the tulips bloomed one warm spell in January, and the azalea flared pink. It is not Springtime, folks, I wanted to whisper into their little veined ears. Go back into hiding. Come out in three months.

When the kids tease Iris for her recycling ways, I say, Have you noticed the weather? It was seventy in December!

They sling their new hot pink purses onto the table. They say, Oh my god, I *love* your clothes.

Thrift store, I say.

Oh my god, I *love* thrift stores.

Vintage, says another.

Meanwhile, they sport their Manolos, their Gucci, their Prada accessories. Tell me about the latest cell phones. Sing me a song of Lilly Pulitzer summer dresses. Don another two hundred dollar blazer. A fat blue silk tie.

Back home, when My Devout Roommate says, It is unseasonably warm, I say, Yes. Global warming.

I drive a car every day. I am no beacon of environmental hope. But here, I stand on a soapbox and say, Haven't you heard of recycling? Don't you people know to eat organic and buy local? I tout the hippies I hated in Colorado. Oh the Consumer Catholics!

What can you do? says My Devout Roommate.

Recycle, I say, for one.

We are in the living room. I'm on the couch, reading my book. Andie comes downstairs, tags jingling. My Devout Roommate stands at the bottom of the stairs. Seps aside and lets Andie pass.

Well, she says, I'm going shopping. Need anything?

No, I say, but Jessica stopped by. She left a note for you; I put it under your door.

Oh, I got it, she says, her voice light.

You've become really close, huh? I say.

She looks at me. Shrugs. I guess, she says. We're *friends*, yeah.

I didn't mean anything by it. Jesus.

Don't take the Lord's name in vain, she says.

I roll my eyes and clear my throat. Look down at my book. Have a good time *shopping*, I say.

She turns and walks up the five stairs in our tiny split-level cottage. Opens the front door. Pulls it shut with a slick bang as the metal slides into the casing.

*   *   *

Weekly Calendar # 10:
  Monday, March 18
    7:18 am Mass
    8:20 am Assembly (Auditorium, Beecher Hall)
    3:00 pm Girls Varsity Soccer at Dorsee Harbor Academy
      Boys & Girls Tennis at Quincy Day
    6:30 pm Student Council Meeting (Barneshead)
    7:00 pm Newspaper Staff Meeting (St. Joseph's Hall)

Assembly begins with a prayer by Brother Timothy, Head of Spiritual Growth. Closes with the sign of the cross: Forehead, Bellybutton, Left Shoulder, Right Shoulder. Then there are the announcements. How did the soccer team fare? Tennis? What were the scores. Which house is winning in the competition for points. Points are given for cleanliness, for community service, for generous acts performed. It's a motivational technique. Assembly goes on with announcements— student groups—French club, Math club, debate team, International Team, and on and on. Next week there will be a fundraiser fair put on by the parents. Donations are welcome. Faculty are encouraged to donate, they say in faculty meeting later, so that it's clear they support the school.

*   *   *

Faculty Meeting, 8 a.m.

The Headmaster stands at the front, navy jacket and a red tie. Khakis. Receding hairline.

Today is the Spring term talk about students who are not doing well. The faculty sit in the tiered wooden chairs that are bolted to the floor. The chairs squeak when they swivel. I sit in the back. I write notes to Talking Man, who sits beside me. Draws more cartoons. A man with big veiny bug eyes, a big wide-open smile.

Allen Parker is having problems in Biology and English, says the Headmaster. He holds a sheet before his eyes. Puts his glasses on to read and takes them off when he looks up. Chews one end of his glasses. *What do his teachers have to say?*

The Bio teacher says, *He's getting a D in my class. He doesn't his homework. He falls asleep. I have to wake him up all the time.*

The English teacher says, *He's always making wisecracks. I've sent him to Dr. Trimble five times this semester.*

Dr. Trimble, the very short, bald Dean of Discipline, says in his deep voice (made over-deep, I think, to compensate for the height), *He's a wiseguy. He doesn't listen. He doesn't seem to care.*

One of the monks, Brother Jacob, says, *Something happened to him this winter. He changed over the break and came back like this. We need to know what happened.*

There is a list of four more boys, and the recommendations are: Study Hall, Suspension, Extra Help at Lunch Hour, Call the Parents, Hold him back a year.

On the other side of me sits Father _____, the angry one. Receding hairline and a wide flat face with a carrot-slice of a nose down the middle. He is unpleasant. His skin has a yellow tint to it. Age spots all over. *He calls us assholes all the time,* say my students, *so we should be able to say that in this class.* I say: No. The students tell me many things they shouldn't. Which teachers they like and, more often, which they hate. *Fuck Mr. _____ for cutting me from the play!* New rule, I say: No swearing about other teachers in this class. No venting about them at all. It puts me in an awkward position. *You don't have to tell them*, they say.

Father _____ teaches math and grades his papers during the meeting, flipping the pages as he goes. Every time a faculty member speaks about troubled students, or the new student survey results which are out, or the upcoming play we should all attend, Father _____ curses. Says: *Shut up you asshole.* Or, *You're full of shit. Sit down.* Or, *As if you've ever even tried that.*

Then, says the Headmaster with his glasses on, there is *Suzanne Walters*, a sophomore. Same problems. Failing Biology. Doing well in History. Doing well in Math, Trigonometry. Failing History of Religion.

She's just not that bright, says someone.

Someone else concurs.

She's nervous, says another, a female teacher. I think it is Mrs. Kennedy, teacher of Science, sitting beside My Devout Roommate, way down front. My One Friend won't look back at me, knows that I'll be fuming. Later, he'll ask if I want to get some coffee, and we'll sit in the coffee shop together and rant. And he'll touch my thigh, and rather than say again that I only want to be friends— saying this, I sense, will make him leave, and I have already given him these hints, doesn't he know? He must know—I'll shift subtly, cross my legs to escape his hand.

Her father thinks she has more potential than she has, says Mr. Clink.

Where's the list of solutions for *her*? Where's the urge to help?

Mr. Jones, in front of us, turns his head, arms crossed, and says under his breath, *She'll make a good mother.*

He laughs. He is in his forties, with a sad-eyed bouffant-blonde wife and four children.

Talking Man laughs and nods. Keeps on drawing the bug-eyed man. Those wiry veins in blue pen, traced over and over.

That's disgusting, I say. But Mr. Jones pretends he did not hear. We won't speak much after this.

*   *   *

Sent: Mar. 12, 2004

Anne,

    Thanks for the invite—drinks sound awesome, but I have dorm duty all weekend. Take care and we will catch up soon about next week.

    Pax et Bunum.
        -- Talking Man

[Pax et Bonum: What St. Francis used to say. Peace and good (or, salvation, say some).]

*

Sent: Mar. 19, 2004

Anne,

This is the game we told you about. It is Top Secret. Some faculty we have not been able to match with a celebrity, but we are pretty close to getting everyone. Feel free to add some suggestions.

      -- Mary Beth Souci

Headmaster Ron Swift – Dick Van Dyke
Andie Swift – Sissy Spacek
He of the Handlebar Mustache – James Gandolfini, Gene Hackman, or Brian Dennehy

Mary Swenson – Talia Shire
Brother Peter – Chewebacca
Abbot Matthew – Nathan Lane
Janet Prenalba –
Thompson Crawford – Andy Kaufman
Al O'Malley – himself OR Peter Boyle
Caroline Renaldo – Cybill Shepherd

*[The list is seven pages long. You love this. You add some names.
You send it back. You are finally part of something here.]*

*   *   *

The Rule of St. Benedict, Prologue

"Listen carefully, my son, to the master's instructions, and attend to them with the ear of your heart. This is advice from a father who loves you; welcome it, and faithfully put it into practice. The labor of obedience will bring you back to him from whom you had drifted through the sloth of disobedience. This message of mine is for you, then, if you are ready to give up your own will, once and for all, and armed with the strong and noble weapons of obedience to do battle for the true King, Christ the Lord.

"First of all, every time you begin a good work, you must pray to him earnestly to bring it to perfection. In his goodness, he has already counted us as his sons, and therefore we should never grieve him by our evil actions. With his good gifts which are in us, we must obey him at all times that he may never become the angry father who disinherits his sons, nor the dread lord, enraged by our sins, who punishes us forever as worthless servants for refusing to follow him to glory..." (Fry 15).

*   *   *

Spray

Skunks everywhere here. You have to watch out when you walk at night. Make some noise to let them know you're coming.

Last week, a skunk walked right into the grocery store. You know what happened then. It got scared. It sprayed like wild. The whole store stank. Couldn't sell the cereal, couldn't sell the bread. Everything that could soak it up, did.

Oh she is laughing, this lady at the counter, about how her dog got sprayed, and she was right behind her dog, and Oh I stink! She says. My God! Can you smell me? It's terrible. We all laugh, too. She says how embarrassing it is, but she loves the attention. We can tell by the way she looks around at us all to see if we are smiling.

People come in here for different reasons. Some of them are lonely, and searching for something to appease their sadness. They want to chat at the counter. They want to tell you about their granddaughter's cold, how it was bad for three days—they called from New Mexico to tell her—and how finally, she got well again. They put their hands in their pockets or they fiddle with their keys, and you know they have no inclination to leave. They are just buying up some time. Face to face. They only want a connection.

This other woman is from Sante Fe, and she says, Oh how I miss the West. She wears a long black coat with a red silhouette of the mountains sprawled across her hips. She says, I wish I could go back. My allergies here are just terrible. My asthma's kicked up again—oh! It's terrible. Just terrible. But my students are here. I teach voice and acting classes. So, you know, I'll be here for a while. But in a few years, I'm going right back. I miss it so much, really.

Yes.

Another man talks about his dogs, these Papillons. Means butterfly. Named for their over-sized wing-like ears with feathered pieces that hang down like palm fronds onto their shoulders. He says how adorable they are, how smart, how they each have their own little children's chair near the window in the living room.

We Had Homework?

they say on Tuesday. Vagrants! Sloths! Visigoths!

After the fourth date:

Just an offer, I said over the phone, to the internet man. He is in Portland. An hour away. We have been dating for two weeks. He is the one they see flushed in my cheeks, not Mr. L. I don't tell them about him, because I'm afraid of getting caught. Caught at my own house with my boyfriend. Ridiculous. But I cannot afford to get fired. He is a lawyer. He wears suits and ties. I've never dated a suit-and-tie man. Usually, it's artists. Cameras slung over their shoulders on our dates, or paint still stuck to their fingertips. Not this one. He parts his hair neatly every morning. He wears socks—matching pairs—every day.

Nothing big, I say. An offer to come.

Well, yeah, that would be—on any other day.

Oh.

I have a big day tomorrow, and I have to get to bed soon. Sleep.

You love your sleep. Of course, that makes sense. A good decision.

But I could come down tomorrow after work.

No, I have plans.

Oh.

But thanks. So, Saturday. I will see you Saturday.

Saturday. Good.

And then we both hang up.

A cold snap tonight, I build a fire with the wood from the Wood Fairy. It crackles in the fireplace. It soothes. I curl up in my old red chair, in thick wool socks, and read. And the rain slates against the wall of windows behind me, and in the bay, the waves crash against the great smooth boulders on the shore. If I walked outside, I would hear them, over and over, a whisper underneath the wind and rain. But I stay inside. I listen to the fire pop. I let it lull me into sleep, and doze until My Devout Roommate walks in at midnight and says, *Whew! Wet one out there!* And even half asleep, I hear how happy she sounds. She hums as she stomps up the stairs. I recognize the hymn: *How great thou art.*

*   *   *

From the Faculty Handbook:

The monks are meant to provide for the students and faculty alike a living example of Christ's devotion. Therefore, they are involved with all aspects of the community, from teaching to athletics to dorm life. It is the monks who lead the evening prayers as well as the daily Masses.

It is the monks who are charged with the spiritual development of the community. They eat with us each day in order to establish a sense of communion. They serve on our board in order to guide us. We trust them to redirect us when necessary. (Handbook 8).

*   *   *

Sent: April 2, 2004
Subject: update to dress code

Please note the addition of Varsity Jackets to the dress code. We allowed them years ago... students stopped wanting to wear them... now they are back. Many students have already received their jackets and will wear them in the spring. Let us know if you have any questions.

Reminder: Spring Warm Weather Dress begins at mid-term (April 20th)

* * *

Unicorn

In the dormitory called St. Bernard's, there is a tapestry on the wall, of a unicorn in a circle, surrounded by rabbits and flowers and deer. It is a small tapestry, thin and fading. The edges are a little tattered. It is mostly brown, and the unicorn is cream-colored. Sits with its legs tucked underneath it, in the pose my little dog often takes, just before settling down for sleep. The unicorn's head is up. It is watching something. Its horn is long and pointed, narrowed to a sharp at the end.

On the other side of the room, there is an altar. A cloth is draped across, hangs down on both sides, narrow on the edges—a runner.

Talking Man's apartment is in the back of this dorm, the far door, and is very well decorated, with everything Just *So*. He has a tier of shelves along one wall, which rise symmetrical on either side, shaping a roof over the couch. The couch matches the oversized chair. Both brown suede, soft hide.

When my little dog runs into his apartment one afternoon, he says, Oh! Oh! Hey there! And he turns frantic to get her out. I call her to the deck and she comes.

Underneath the deck, there are often skunks. Beware, says Talking Man, when I leave, full of red wine. I like to jangle my keys, he says, to warn them. Like bear bells, I say, in Colorado.

Bear bells. Nothing like skunk keys, really.

If the unicorn bleeds, its blood is clear. Its blood can give you life forever.

Maybe this is why the Catholics love the unicorn—eternal life.

In medieval times, we were tortured in the Spanish Inquisition. This is what my One Friend tells me at my house one night. Really? I say. The Catholics? I thought the Spanish Inquisition was some other religion?

Nope, he says. Dominicans. Catholics.

I knew this once.

The Dominican monks wear white robes.

Well I guess the Catholics got theirs in the Holocaust, I say.

My One Friend laughs. Sorry, I say. I take that back. Sorry, God! I shout up to the kitchen ceiling. There are ants crawling on the floor here and there, because we have an ant problem. Carpenter ants that should not have been born until Spring. But it is too warm here now. No real winter. Not even any snow on the ground.

The Unicorn is pure and good. White. The magic of the horn.

The Chinese say the unicorn was seen five thousand years ago. The Greeks knew of the unicorn. The Bible mentions it, sometimes good, sometimes evil. The unity of God and Jesus, the unicorn's horn and body. The Father, the Son, the Holy Spirit. A trinity.

There's a Jewish tale says the unicorn was banished from the ark for being too pushy. Tossed into the sea, the couple learned to swim. They became narwhals. Horned whales.

Narwhals look like dolphins—gentle eyes and round noses—and white, too, with that brilliant horn on their foreheads. Mesmerized in the fifth grade, I learned all about them and wrote a book. Now I hear the narwhals will be the first to go when global warming gets us. The ocean will be too warm. They are reclusive. They are hard to find. They like the cold depths.

Queens in France—Elizabeth the First—wore the unicorn horn, which was so valuable only a queen could afford it. She wore it around her neck for protection. But now, they say, it was the tusk of a narwhal she wore.

Maybe the narwhal gave as much protection, anyway, as any unicorn could have. Just as rare—swimming through the dark depths with the horn, with the white body, gentle.

Everything in the sea a mystery to us, and we fill it with our filth. Along the shore, trash washes up. Bottles and plastic and pieces of things that were used once, by someone, miles and miles away. The tide carries it all, dutifully, to shore, tosses it up like a dog playing fetch—*Is this what you were looking for?* Toss it back to fetch again.

In another tapestry, the unicorn is surrounded by dogs, splashing through a river. The dogs wear colored collars made of embroidered fabric. The men wear pantaloons and carry spears. The unicorn's eyes are wide and white-rimmed, and he knows—of course, he knows—that he is trapped. This is the end. All these dogs and all these men, there is no chance this one will survive. A unicorn can kill any beast with that horn, but in the face of this hunting party, it has no defense.

The unicorn will be killed, and the men will take home the horn. Maybe the hide, too, maybe not. Maybe the body will simply be left behind. The horn is all they need. They will show it to their friends, celebrate with a feast, hold it in their hands. Passing it from one to the other. The next day, the next week, they will sell it to someone very rich, who will drill a hole through it and wear it around her neck. For protection.

So the world goes. So ends the hunt.

*   *   *

Mrs. Souci says she did not see it coming, Mr. Souci's death. Mr. Souci is the one who found Mister Hester. Who killed himself. Mrs. Souci says, When Luke started teaching here, something happened, something faded from him. But I've stayed because they have been good to me. Soon, I will leave. My daughters and I will leave. I will go to live with my brother in Connecticut. Luke became sad. Luke drifted off, and then he died, she says. She does not say: Killed himself. She does not say: I know the rumor of his affair. She does not say if it was true or not. Was he sleeping with Mister Hester? I don't ask. Mr. Souci died three years ago, so most of the students here did not know the men. Only the seniors. And even they call the English teacher Mister Hester now, as in Hester Prynne. They pretend it is a joke. But it is because they are afraid, or it is a way of saying: This place, this place will get you if you are not careful. His nickname a warning.

*   *   *

Sprinkled on Top

Four days before Spring Vacation, Kathryn says, My friends sprinkle codeine on top of their pot when they smoke it.

Kathryn, I say, inappropriate.

She was talking about her friends, not her, says Ruth.

Enough pot talk, I say. It is a test, with her. Always pushing pushing.

Iris says, Codeine is really addictive.

It is, I say, it's horrible for you. Very addictive. You could die from that.

Whatever, says Kathryn. I don't do it. My *friends* do.

She looks at Steven and grins. Steven grins back. They have become comrades.

Kathryn, I say to her on her way out, One more mention of drugs in this class will land you in Mr. Trimble's office.

She rolls her eyes and walks away. Says as she goes, You won't do *that*, all singsong.

*   *   *

In college, I stopped going to church. Never went back. Except when I was home for the holidays. Then we went *as a family*. But three years later, when all the news about the priests came out, even my parents stopped going for awhile. Even they realized how much sickness was embedded. How they silenced those victims for so long. Denied anything was wrong. Simply transferred the offending priests. Who were in fact criminals. Who had ruined people's lives. Three boys in our town came forward. Not because of the young, cool priest but because of the old priest. One of those boys killed himself. Did not leave a note or explanation, but people made connections. And they gathered at the base of the mountain in the springtime, and held signs and protested at the church, at the rectory. They'd been betrayed. For years.

*   *   *

Headmaster

He is a bald-white man with a nodding head. A grin most of the time. Going: ab-badabadbadaba.

He lives in a house right on the bay with his very tall wife. She wears long skirts every day, with tights. She huffs through the woods to the campus, a half mile walk, because she's been on a diet. Lost forty-five pounds. Says she does the Points system—Weight Watchers. Goes to Portland twice a week for meetings. It's about the support, she says, the support system.

They have six grown daughters.

They have a fireplace that blows out smoke most of the winter, and a stout pine tree with colored lights in the front yard, which faces nothing but some trees and the water. Their yard falls right into the bay. You can only see the chimney from campus.

They have been together thirty years. Such a long time. As long as I have been alive.

She says: We put the lights on the tree for the sailors. You know, on the barges.

Quahoggers, I say.

Yeah, right.

I have learned some things about Maine. For example: If you see a moose, don't run. Stand still. If it races for you, try to climb a tree. If you see black or brown bear, stand very tall and wave your arms. Up north, there are fewer of the very rich than in the south, where the tourists congregate. Kennebunkport. Ogunquit. Many rich and many poor. A blue-collar state. (Talking Man says: I love it because it's blue-collar. But because Talking Man is getting his PhD and talks about his IQ, this sounds kind of condescending. I am of this place, he says. So. What this means is: he can say what he likes.)

The Headmaster throws a party for the people. It is catered by the dining hall people, who are very accommodating, who do everything they can for the people who work here, for the kids. Special meals for special diets and allergies, and waiting for the stragglers, and letting us use the refrigerator when ours went dead at the cottage.

At the party, we all get drunk. There is a bar, and a spread of food, and the Headmaster's wife, says, *Come see our daughter's rooms*, and takes us on a tour of the house. The house is an old colonial, with four rooms upstairs and a master bedroom downstairs. Four of the girls shared a room until the oldest two went to college. *Esther, Dinah, Ruth, Delilah, Leah, Hannah.*

You must love the Old Testament, I say.

She looks at me with her head cocked. Her long, long blonde hair falling down her back. She sways back and forth, so thin. Well, she says, Yes, I suppose.

We walk back downstairs. The stairs creak. I hold the banister. I've been drinking rum.

This house, she says, was built in seventeen-ninety-two by the same man who built the Portland Lighthouse, you know.

Really? I say. That's old.

Oh, yes, she says, the oldest lighthouse in Maine. We got engaged there, Henry and I.

How sweet, I say.

It was, she says. He completely surprised me. It was sunset.

I turn to see her, but the stairway is too dim. We are back downstairs, where all the people talk and laugh and eat and drink. Clusters of teachers and staff and their husbands and wives.

I walk up to My One Friend. He's scooping potato salad onto a paper plate. Has been here for two hours already, drinking whiskey.

How's it going? I say.

Great! he says. Great! How are you?

He tilts forward, tilts back. He's wearing a navy button-down, tucked into jeans. A brown leather belt. Brown shoes. I smell the whiskey on his breath.

Good, I say. I laugh a little.

He stares at me, potato salad spoon in his hand. The plate in the other hand. His eyes fuzzy behind his glasses.

You know, he says. He raises the spoon. You look pretty tonight.

Thanks, I say.

One of the teachers behind him, Mrs. Souci, turns and smiles at us. Thinks this is young love. She is in her thirties and already a widow, with a two year old daughter.

I raise my hand to say hi. Feel myself go red. She waves back.

Here, let me. I reach for the spoon and the plate, and take them from his hands, and finish serving the salad.

What else do you want? Some ham?

I turn back to the table and fork the ham onto the plate. Deviled eggs. Salad. Bread.

He stands behind me, scratching his neck. I turn back to him with the plate. The ceiling is low, and makes the room feel full.

Good, he says, good.

Take it, I say.

He takes the plate from me.

Let's sit outside for a bit.

Okay, he says, and we weave through the clusters of people to the porch, to the brick wall at the far end where no one's sitting.

We sit side by side, facing the patio, the sliding doors that lead back inside.

There's so much food, he says. I love this party. Every year, the food's amazing. And open bar.

That's why I came, I say. I laugh. Sip my rum and coke.

He eats his ham. Picks up the whole piece with his fork and bites off pieces. Want some? he says.

No, thanks.

I watch the Headmaster's wife push her hair over her shoulder, and nod at something My Devout Roommate's saying. My Devout Roommate has lost weight, has been running, walking, biking everywhere. Some kind of personal revolution. No more Swedish fish on the couch. Jessica, the baloney-curled math teacher, straight out of college, walks up beside them, and touches hips—a graze that lingers—with My Devout Roommate, who is gesticulating. Telling some story. Her hair in a ponytail tied with a red bow. Catholics love bows.

At the far end of the room, Talking Man is talking to Brother Timothy and Mr. Jones, and Abbot Paul is laughing with Mrs. Newell.

I feel a hand on my cheek. I turn.

Anne, he says. Anne.

He looks at me a while, his hand on my face, and for a moment, I think about it. Think about this. He is kind. He is funny sometimes. He means well. He has helped me through this year.

But I feel nothing with his hand on my face. I do not want to kiss him, not really. And just as I think: No, he leans in fast and does it himself. The taste of ham.

I push him back without thinking. Too hard.

He sits there for a minute, watching me. His eyes blue and hurt behind his glasses, his back curved with his slouch. He never got used to being so tall. He puts his hand back on his leg.

Sorry, he says. He looks down. Puts his plate on the wall with his other hand.

No, I say, I didn't mean to do that. But, you know, I'm seeing someone now.

He nods. I know, he says. But what about this?

I don't say anything. I hear the Headmaster's chortle. See Mrs. Souci watching us through the sliding glass door. Gossip for tomorrow's brunch in the dining hall—*did you see Mr. L kiss Ms. James? Did you see them making out?*—how word will spread across campus, all the way down to my students.

He stands up then, and turns and climbs over the wall, and runs across the field toward campus, legs kicking fast.

Wait! I say. I turn and holler to him. Wait up!

But he's already gone into the darkness.

*   *   *

Into the woods and then the fields, the wide green fields, that have been cleared for pretty views, that lead to campus. And on the way, a row of animals made from bushes. Topiary. In the middle of the field, a hallway to follow back to school. Stand inside and look at the animals and listen to the ocean. Who made this? Brother Timothy. His hobby, his art. What looks like whimsy is devotion.

Benedictine monks are given time to devote to their art. Time to read. Time to pray. (Gail says, Sounds like a good deal. Sit around reading and thinking and making stuff? Sign me up.) Brother Joseph says, We need each of these roles in the church; we are crumbling because we don't have enough people praying anymore. Not enough nuns and monks, who contemplate and pray. We need that prayer to support the priests who do the service with the public. So, out of balance, we get this sickness (this sickness means "the pedophiles").

An elephant with an arched trunk, a lion with a wide round mane, a small Scottish terrier, a ten-foot sea monster—serpentine spiked tail—a guard at the end of the row, and then, in the center of the row, where it widens and arches out on either side to make a circle with a stone bench for sitting: a unicorn. Up on her hind legs, rearing. Ready to run off as soon as she lands. She is always there, hooves grabbing at the air. She is always on her way down.

*   *   *

Post –

The next day, I am hungover from the party, all the teachers are. Slogging in to brunch haggard and dark-eyed. We get to start late today, at nine instead of seven, thanks to the party.

I called My One Friend three times last night, and he did not call back. He was not at breakfast. I called Talking Man, and he talked about St. Thomas of Aquinas for awhile, and his writings, and how it is a book I might like, and how in his Life Skills class today he taught the rhythm method, and I said, You're kidding, right? That's a horrible thing to teach high school students. And he said it's been proven effective, it has, and it's something I should learn more about.

Kathryn comes to class and pulls out her pen. Everyone else settles into their chairs, the creak of wood and metal, of the attached desks folding down onto their laps, the rustle of papers and of searching for a pen.

I don't have one, says Steven. Can I borrow one, Kathryn?

I have one, says Abigail across the circle. Here. She holds one out to him.

But Kathryn is right beside him, and says, Here, Steven.

It is not a pen. It is a joint. A white rolled joint.

Steven looks at it and covers his mouth, laughs.

Oh my God, Kathryn, you're so stupid, says Abigail. Put it away.

Um, says Iris, Kathryn what is *that.*

Ruth just sits there stone-faced, shaking her head. Puts her head into one hand. Maria giggles.

I am seeing red. Head splitting down the center with my hangover, and now this. Pushing, pushing.

Okay, Kathryn, I say, Off to Mr. Trimble.

I feel like a traitor. I am a traitor. But what else can I do? A joint in class?

She snickers. Yeah, right, she says. I'm not going up there.

Oh, yes you are, I say. And now I'm angry and I mean it. Go, I say. Now.

She scoffs and says, All right, fine, I'll go. I don't care. It's not even real. It's a fake joint. I was just playing a joke. She stands up and breaks it in half, and there's nothing inside—it's just paper. She throws it on the floor, right at my feet, and reaches down and grabs her backpack, and walks across the linoleum floor to the door, and opens it and slams it behind her.

All the other students sit silent. Saying nothing. They glance at each other. They don't move.

Fuck! she shouts from the hallway, and stomps down the stairs. We hear her footsteps fading.

I look out the window, and the sun is shining, and the bay is all prettied up—tilting sailboats and green oaks and birches around the shore and the pines all sparkly in the sunshine. Tulips in the gardens around campus. Pretty red tulips.

*　　　*　　　*

Sent: April 10, 2004
Dear Faculty and Staff,
Please join us for a Blessing of the Ground, Saturday April 12, at 10 a.m., to commemorate the breaking of ground for the new science building, which, as you know, will include four new labs and seven classrooms fitted with smart technology. We're very grateful to the PR folks who made this possible through their fundraising efforts. Thank you to all faculty, alumni, and staff who contributed to the fund. The ceremony will be followed by a special brunch buffet in the dining hall.

Headmaster Swift

*　　　*　　　*

Bury a statue of Saint Joseph in the ground in front of your house, upside-down, and your house will sell quickly. You can buy it online. For nine ninety-nine.

Saint Francis of Paola will protect the sailors and the seamen. Quahoggers. Clammers. Lobster boats.

Saint Christopher will help you find things. When I was small, I was at Katie O'Malley's house, and her mother lost the keys, and we walked all over the house saying, "Oh, St. Christopher, please help us find the keys." At last, they turned up in one of the built-in bookshelves. Then we could go upstairs and play Battleship.

*   *   *

Art

How is your collage? says Brother Matthew, the sculpture and photography teacher. How is it going?

It's all right, I say. Getting there.

We are sitting on the stone wall in front of the Arts Building, a break in the sunshine before I go inside.

So, he says, this has been good for you? This time?

Yes, I say. Hard, but good.

Hard—how so?

Oh, I say, You know, high school students. I laugh.

He nods. They can be difficult, he says.

How's your sculpting?

Come with me, he says, and leads me inside.

We go to the back of the building, to the room with the wide row of windows that face the sea, where the students have their their sculpture classes (photography is in the basement), and he shows me his work.

These are the reliefs I've been working on, he says.

They're all hands. Hands reaching out. Hands crossed over each other. Hands cupped. Strong hands, like his own, with long fingers.

He goes to the wall and turns on the track lights, so we can see how they'll look in the gallery, when they're shown.

They look good, I say. Beautiful.

He moves one of the reliefs to the center of the table. Suddenly, in this light, it changes. The hands reach out. The hands are all full of grace, the fingers long and reaching. The fingers waiting to hold.

Oh, I say, wow.

I used to make a lot of money for these, he says, I had plenty of commissions.

And now?

Now I teach, he says, and make these for free, or for churches.

I can't imagine, I say. I shake my head, still looking at the hands.

What? Giving them away?

I nod.

It's in His name, he says, and gestures up again.

He gives me a business card, with his name and the cross on the front, and a picture of one of the reliefs on the back. Two cupped hands, one under the other. I imagine what it would be like to have his faith, to give away my work for God's sake.

I walk up to my students thinking about this: light and shadows. What can change, and what cannot.

*   *   *

A workshop with a Benedictine nun, for one whole day. Saturday. Just before vacation. Do we have to go? Yes. It is required. The nun knows these monks from something in the past, some affiliation, and now she's here to talk about the mission and duties of a Benedictine school. We are stewards of the land, she says. Place is very important, we have a strong sense of place, grounded in place. She says, Here are the hallmarks of a Benedictine Education, the love of learning, desire for good: 1) Prayer. Everyone knows or is learning how to pray. 2) Obedience, listening, paying attention to others. Students need quiet and leisure that demands no activity and no productivity of them. This will make them more present in themselves, and to everything around them. 3) Stability—in relationships and community. There is wisdom to be found in the faithfulness of the daily. 4) Discipline. Daily regular practice. Disciplined students learn autonomy and the ability to establish relationships with others. 5) Sense of stewardship. An awareness of the goodness of the natural world. 6) Humility. This, she says, is St. Benedict's word for wisdom. Accept yourself as you are, both gifted and limited, and teach students to do the same. Embrace our strengths and recognize the gifts of others. 7) Support for one another. Communities are weakened where support is withheld. 8) Hospitality. Cultivate in the young a spirit of hospitality. Benedictines recognize the blessing of receiving a stranger and the blessing they can offer. When a stranger comes with something strange to say; they may be a messenger of God. You must consider their message. Be open to all the gifts of strangers and the adjustments their presence may require us to make. 9) Love. Mutual love finds its expression in patience with one another. Elders are wise in love and know how to overlook foibles.

63

We live in an international culture of violence that expresses itself in verbal, physical abuse—Benedictines practice love. 10) A commitment to the transformation of our own, true humanity advances us on the path to our truest selves.

The nun says, Now you'll be in groups, and ask yourselves if St. Christopher's School is following these tenets and how, and if there's room for improvement, and how. Discuss. Come back and report.

You are assigned to Group #5. Mrs. Souci leads. Says, Are we good stewards? You say, We don't even recycle here. True, she says. And all those trees we cut down! you say. True, she says. But when we meet in the big group again, she reports back that we are good stewards, we have seaside clean-up day and replant any tree that is cut down and conserve on water—this is what every group says, how good this place is at all those tenets, all those rules. We do them all! This was a workshop for patting ourselves on the back, you see.

Afterwards, say to Talking Man: It isn't all bad, the ideas, some of them sound good. Oh, he says, She got it all wrong. Those are not the Tenets. We learned them in Seminary. He laughs. We talked about that with Brother Matthew in our group. He says, She doesn't know; she is just a nun. He says.

*   *   *

Hagiography: The lives of saints. Translated in the twelfth century from Latin so that everyone could understand. There were three of four different Saint Franceses, not just the animal lover.

Patron Saints of this and that.
Pater. Father. A song I remember, learning Latin: Mater waaageet! Pater waaaageet!

The Haitians have spirits whose names are the same as the Catholic saints. The Catholic saints were all white people. The Haitian spirits were never people. But, when enslaved people had their time for worship and the white masters came around, the slaves would pretend they were talking about the Catholic saints. So the saints

were a way of disguising the voodoo. What they were really doing.
A mask, a shield, a guise: some form of protection.

*   *   *

Guitar

We have a class party the day before Spring Vacation, and my students come to our house and I play the guitar. Bad songs in a bad tune. I make up the words as I go. The students don't know, at first, if it's all right to laugh. They look at each other sidelong.

It's okay, I say, I know these are bad. Go ahead and laugh.

So then they do. Steven pulls the pillow closer to him on the couch and his face wrinkles up and Iris throws her head back and Abigail lies back on the floor and does her giggle and Grace looks to Abigail and laughs just a little.

Flipping through my photo albums while I made them lunch, they found the picture of me skiing with Danny. Kissing on the chairlift. Ed had taken it from the chair in front of us. The weekend we were engaged. Just after he took the picture, Ed said, teasing, Aw, sweet love. We laughed.

Oh, God, I said. I forgot that picture's in there.

Don't worry, Ms. James, says Iris, I was only embarrassed for a second and now I'm over it.

Well, says Abigail, how old are you?

Thirty, I say.

I'm seventeen. So that's thirteen years. It's not that big a difference. You're not that much older.

Okay, I say, sure.

He's cute, says Ruth, but you can do better, Ms. James.

Thanks, Ruth, I say.

What happened? says Abigail.

Oh, you know, I say. I swash my hand in the air. I don't say: We were living together in Crested Butte. For a year. We'd been together three. And then, come winter, he sort of disappeared, a silence that lasted weeks then months. Would not talk to me anymore, would not talk about it. Went into this silence. What did I do? I asked at first. And then I said: You are depressed, you need some help. But more and more, he was away, and when he came home, he'd smile and have dinner and say almost nothing. We were supposed to get married last summer. But I broke up with him. Said goodbye to Gail and Ed and our friends. Moved here. End of story.

Okay, says Abigail. She doesn't want to talk about it. Iris, how's *Grant*?

Iris blushes. Grant is her new boyfriend, who goes to Glick Day Academy, half an hour away. Good, she says.

They talk about who is dating whom on campus and who just broke up and who should get together. All these girls circled up on the living room floor.

Do you guys know what safe sex is? I say, and they all blush and say, *Ms. James*, and I say, Well, of course you should abstain from sex. But, you know, condoms help protect you from STD's and pregnancy, just for future reference.

They laugh, and turn away, and Iris says, Okay, Ms. James.

Grace and Iris wander upstairs, linger in my painting room, where the collage is strung up with clothespins. I hope they don't go into my bedroom. Go and get them, I say to Abigail, and make sure they're not doing anything bad.

They tromp back down together. It is raining out. They wear boots.

Sometimes I feel so lonely, says Steven from the corner. He sits in the tall red wingchair, a pillow in his lap.

Oh, say the girls, Steven. You can talk with us. Tell us what you think. Who do you have a crush on?

No, says Steven.

Do you miss Kathryn? I say.

Yeah, he says.

The students look at him and then back up at me. Kathryn's been suspended for two days. Because of the joint incident. The students are still a little angry with me; it subsides and then rises up again. I feel badly for her, days before break. I didn't want to send her to Mr. O'Malley. But she kept pushing and pushing, and then, on impulse, I did it. And once I said it, I could not back down (I told myself) she had to go. We both dug in our heels. I called My One Friend to talk about it, knowing he's heard by now, but he won't call me back. It rang and rang and rang. No voicemail this time. I called Talking Man and Mrs. Souci, and both said: Of course you had to do that. Of course you did, should have a long time ago. Lucky she got this far. But they are staunch. They would say this.

She made a bad choice, I say. I'm sorry she's not here, too.

It's the high school teacher response. *Choices—good and bad.* But still, she should not have been suspended for that. She could have been given, instead, study hall this week, or no soccer game on Friday—anything else would have sufficed. It wasn't *actually* pot.

Did you hear about Allen Wall? says Grace, sitting on the blue chair in the corner.

No, I say, who's he?

He got kicked out for smoking pot in the boathouse last year.

Yeah, says Abigail, but Tom Jenkins and Lena Magfish got caught *doing it*, and nothing happened to them.

They weren't doing it, says Linda. It was just a blowjob.

Just a blowjob? says Steven. He giggles.

Thanks for filling me in, I say. Moving on.

What's our final project? says Iris.

And I tell them about the painting we'll all do together, as big as the wall in the classroom, one long canvas, a collaborative painting with words sewn into it.

Cool, says Iris.

Yeah, say Abigail and Linda and Ruth.

I feed them pasta salad and grilled chicken and corn on the cob. It was supposed to be a barbeque, but instead we cooked inside. The rain falls off the roof in big sheets. The bay is frothy. No sailboats. Just the big tankers and the fishing boats. Lobster boats with the traps cast up on the side.

Iris says, Thanks, Ms. James. This must have been really expensive. We can pay you for this.

It's okay, I say. Don't sweat it.

Yeah, thanks, they all say.

Do you like living with Ms. Dinse? says Steven.

Sure, I say.

That means no, says Abigail.

Yeah, says Maria.

Yes, I do, I say. She's fine.

Then it's time to get back into the car and go to campus. Eight of them in my car, not safe. Two on laps in the front seat, three in the back, and two in the way-back. Station wagon. On the way in, Steven bumps his head.

I knew someone was going to get hurt! I say. This is dangerous to drive this way.

He's fine, says Ruth. The damage was done long ago.

No, says Iris, he hit it really hard. I saw.

On what? I say. I jump out and run to the way-back to see. The rain falls cold against my neck. Splatters on the driveway. Shouts its way down the hill to the ocean in fat rivulets.

Steven holds his head.

Are you okay? Are you bleeding?

No, not bleeding he says. Ow.

You need to go to the infirmary. When we get back.

I can't, he says, I have a class.

No, you need to go. I'll write you a note.

It's okay. I'm fine.

I think he's okay, says Abigail.

I close the door on them and run to the front seat. Two of them have a test. My little yellow dog climbs into my lap from the driveway, all wet. Sits there while we drive.

Shit, I say in the driveway, the headmaster. His old Beamer coming toward us.

Iris tries to cover Abigail. Look like one head, one person.

I wave hello as if there's nothing amiss.

He waves back.

Shit, I say, there's Babette. She's walking towards us in a trench coat, with an umbrella overhead. She'll surely see into the car. Busted by Mrs. Dregville. The science teacher, who is in her forties and single and very cranky.

Oh, says Iris, *Babette*. I had to spend seventeen hours with her last week.

I know, I say, I know.

Stupid science experiment. It didn't even work. The plants didn't even grow.

68

We drive on, past the Administration building and the wide sloping lawns. Stop at the brick Tudor.

They pile out at the classroom building. Goodbye!

They pile out at the art building. Goodbye!

I let them out at their dorm. Goodbye!

And then the car is empty, and I drive back to my messy kitchen with my little yellow dog. The front door is swung wide open when I get there, rain blowing into the entryway. The rug is all wet. Whoever left last, I think.

We are on vacation now, I say to my dog. I sit down on the couch, and sleep.

　　　　※　　　　※　　　　※

In high school, I had to go on a retreat with that CCD group. We went to some whitewashed place, houses clustered together— maybe a hospital once—now empty. There were bunk beds in one of the buildings, and we slept there together, and went for walks during the day, and had meetings at night. I went to confession one afternoon because we all had to go, and it was a dark room with two chairs in it, not a vestibule but a makeshift confession room. I didn't have any sins I wanted to report, so I said, *Forgive me, Father for I have sinned.* And he said, *It's 'Bless me.' I cannot forgive you.* I corrected myself, and then made up some sins. Lies I'd told, friends I'd betrayed. I made it up because I didn't want to have to sit there for very long. *You sin like this because you feel badly about yourself,* he said, *I want you to picture those people's faces and let them wash over you and think about how you have hurt them. Three Hail Mary's and fifteen Our Father's.* And then I walked into another room where other people were praying, and the girl who came to school drunk whispered, kneeling, How many did you get? And I told her, and she said, Ooooh, as if I was very bad. What about you? I said. And she said, Two and two.

Another time, we went to this big Catholic convention, which was held in a giant meeting hall with ten meeting rooms and an auditorium that held a thousand. And a priest gave a talk about that song, *Walking on Broken Glass*, and how it's about God's love, how that's what everything's about if we listen for it. And every time I

69

hear that song now, I think of him, in his glasses and his collared shirt and black pants, skinny arms at the front of the room, trying to connect with us kids. And how some of the kids loved it, loved the whole thing, were really into it, laughed and talked and carried around canvas tote bags with their church name printed on them, and I thought: brain-washed. All about God, he said. It's all about God.

*   *   *

Apr. 13, 2004
Dear Faculty,

Please excuse the following students from classes Tuesday, Apr. 17 and Wednesday, Apr. 18, for dress rehearsal. If you have any questions, do not hesitate to contact me.

Mrs. Parker
Drama and Music
St. Christopher's, Pawtucksey, ME

*   *   *

Internet Man

He is funny. He plays the guitar, classical, and we sit in the sunshine on Sunday and he sings. Like we are hippies. The sun is shining, and the yard is green, and the trees bow around us, making shade.

He stops and looks up at the trees. After a minute, he says, Is there a piano here?

In the Admin Building, I say, Yeah.

Can we play it?

I guess, I say. But if we go to the Admin Building they'll see us.

So?

Well.

You'll get in trouble? He grins, a sly grin up one side. We are in high school, suddenly, the two of us. He was raised Catholic, too. He likes this idea.

All right, I say.

We stand up and the wind blows off the bay. A cool wind. I turn and look down at the water. Across the bay, the lighthouse. A sailboat rocks. I hear someone laughing by the shore, a sound that floats up. And then someone hollers, a shriek, a splash, and laughter again.

Where's your roommate? he says.

I think she's by the water, I say.

He leans in, kisses me. He has dark hair and is almost the same height as me—an inch taller—and he wears old jeans that are all tattered at the hem, not suits anymore (says he'd just come from the office each time we'd met the first two weeks), and t-shirts washed soft. He runs every morning, and races some weekends, all over New England. Tries to convince me to train with him. Ha, I laugh. He lives in Portland, is a lawyer, owns a coffee shop. Brings me bags of coffee beans when he comes up. A month now we've known each other. One sweet young month. His name is BP, short for what he won't say. His friends called him by his initials in high school, told him he was bubonic plague. Drinking Beast Light at the parties. He grew up here, in Portland. He loves it here. Could never leave.

Up from the water comes My Devout Roommate, and with her is Jessica. They don't see us. BP is folding the blanket, facing the other way. I hear him shake it out. And as I watch My Devout Roommate and Jessica, in their bathing suits with towels tied around their waists, emerge from the shrubs that line the trail, into this spot of sunshine on the lawn: Jessica touches My Devout Roommate's shoulder. Runs her hand through her hair and says something, and My Devout Roommate turns to her, sees only her (not us, further back on the lawn, in the shade), and in that bit of dappled sunshine, they kiss.

No. Way. I say.

BP turns. What? he says. Oh, it's her. Because they've pulled away now and have turned to us, and BP raises his hand and waves. Hey guys, he says. Nice day, huh?

They don't wave back. They stand very still. And then they turn to the house, and walk to the front door where I can't see them, and slip fast inside. I hear the latch click.

Ready? says BP.

Yeah, I say, and we walk to the path Jessica and my roommate just walked, and go down to the shore, all rocks, and walk its edge to campus. BP carries the blanket, and picks up a stone to skip, five staccato jumps across the water, and tells me where he buys his coffee beans and how I need to meet his dog soon. We'll have to see if they like each other, he says, Green and Andie.

Your dog's name is Green?

Yeah, he says. He laughs. I let my nephew name him.

How old was your nephew?

Three. It was a bad idea.

I laugh.

When we get to the Admin Building, it is quiet. No students searching the Mail Room for their mail, or in the office where Brother Joseph keeps the Tin Box of money. No flip-flops (leather, of course, not rubber) smacking the floor, or children calling out to each other. It is quiet. The wood floor creaks. I look into the room with the couches, where parents sit sometimes while students interview or tour, or while they speak with teachers about their student's progress. Couches I sat on to speak with parents.

I hear someone walking in the offices upstairs, heavy footsteps. Maybe the Blockhead. Maybe Mr. O'Malley.

I turn right, into the auditorium. Only fifty chairs, not enough for the whole school. The weekly meetings are held in the Humanities building, where the big auditorium sits on the first floor, and can hold four hundred. Orange cloth seats. A matching curtain. Every week the Headmaster stands up there with his announcements, and then the student groups with theirs. Who won which games, what were the scores, what clubs are meeting which days this week, special Masses, and on and on.

We walk to the front of the room where the grand piano sits glossed up.

Ooooh, he says, it's a Steinway.

I know, I say. An alumnus from Kennebunk donated it this fall. Keeps his yacht at the club and people say he has an upright in the cabin. I wish I could play.

You could accompany me on guitar, he says.

I laugh. Right. You play. Play something.

And then he sits and says, Chopin, and plays a tune made for nighttime, and I sit in one of the chairs and listen. The way his hands move up and down the keys. A lawyer-coffee-shop-man who plays piano and guitar.

You're an anomaly, I say, and he looks at me and grins. Raises his eyebrows. Hot, he says.

I hear a creak behind me, and turn to see Mr. O'Malley in the doorway, and he waves hello, and I wave back, and then he ducks away again, and BP laughs. He keeps on playing. I lean back in my chair and listen and smile.

*   *   *

*Mrs. Souci says that she'll never fall in love again, says it was her and Luke and that was it. But, I say, it's been three years; maybe— She shakes her head. She says, No, and her lips are pinched and there is no talking past this line, no talking about what happened, about the rumors or the hurt underneath it, the truth of it. She looks up and smiles. Says, But **you**—you will find something good.*

*   *   *

Shadowed

That night, My Devout Roommate is not home. I don't know where she is, but the house is so quiet and it is so late that I know she isn't coming back tonight. The house is silent and full of shadows. BP and I walk inside. Have been walking on the beach all day. Drove down to Portland and sat by the lighthouse, the lighthouse where the Headmaster and his wife got engaged. It is beautiful and white and old, with a red roof, and the wind slides around it. We picked up Green, a blue heeler, and introduced her to little yellow Andie, and they chased each other across the lawn around the lighthouse. Until the keeper came and told us to get those dogs on leashes, please. All right.

BP drove us back here in his old jeep, roofless, wool sweater pulled tight around me, the dogs in the back with their tongues lolling. And I thought, It is vacation, and no one is around, and no one will see us, and they won't really *enforce* that rule. He can stay over. I am not afraid of them.

Now the dogs race into the house, claws clicking on the wood floor. They run down the five steps to the living room, lap water from the dish, taking turns. Lie down on the floor, panting.

We are home and it is quiet. The ocean sloshes at the shore. The wind blows just a little. We slip upstairs to bed.

3

Return

The week went by like that—easy and sweet. Lying in the sunshine, sleeping late in the morning, spending time in bed. BP would go to work in the morning and come up at night, or I'd go to his house. Either way. If we stayed in Portland, we drank coffee at his shop in the mornings and walked to buy bread from the bakery.

My Devout Roommate left a note on the kitchen table downstairs. It said, *I'm off to see my family in New Hampshire. I'll be back next week.*

So I wouldn't talk to her about what happened for a while. And BP and I were free to do as we liked.

But finally, Monday came, and, still lying in bed with BP, I heard her come home, shut the door to her room, and then leave twenty minutes later. I thought: She will keep my secret because I am keeping hers. I'd let my guard down; she saw BP's car in the driveway. She knew we were in bed.

Then BP left for Portland, and it was time to go back to school. Back to the students, who, I would see, were even worse than they were before the break.

*   *   *

In the sea, bobbing on the surface, are the buoys. Jump into the water, follow the ropes down to the floor. Traps. Lobsters. Blue and greenish-brown, with great wide claws (if they are old) and skinny spider legs. Crustacean. Also crustaceans: crabs and craw-daddies. Trash-eaters. Floor-walkers. Scavengers. Once they were food for the poor. Now: delicacy. Twenty dollars apiece, claws banded shut. Echinoderm: Sea urchins, starfish, sea horse. If a starfish loses a leg, it will grow a new one (like a salamander's tail). The male seahorse carries the babies in his pouch. That sweet curled tail. Bivalves: Oysters, clams and scallops. Here, the clams are Quahogs. Oysters and clams dig down; scallops sit on the sand. Walk on the sand and see the water-bubbles come up from clam's holes. Breathing out. An oyster starts off male and becomes female. Shells for protection: bivalves, two halves. When cooked, the slender necks emerge (not really necks but feet).

Pawtucksey, ten minutes north, was a fishing town, built in the seventeen hundreds by men and women who made their living from the sea. Old slanting colonials side by side, natural shingles faded to gray, or slats painted bright colors: red, watermelon, robin's egg blue. Hardy.

On the way to campus, sit by the church, the arching lawn that falls to the rocks and the pines and the sea, and there is the smell of incense floating out, leftover from Monday morning Mass, and the salty sea smell, mixes together, and down below, deep deep in the water, the lobsters crawl, feeling with antennae, and the oysters suck in gallons of water seeking food, and the whales migrate north—in breeding season, calling out the moan-language we try to decode. It is a love song. From the male to the female. It is a song to woo. It is the Humpback song. A long and lovely longing.

There is also the Minke, and the Right Whale, the most endangered of all. "Right" for hunting. Easy prey, slow swimmer. Only three hundred or so left. A big lower jaw.

Cetacean: Whales, including narwhals—toothed whales. Narwhal meaning corpse whale. Eat cod and shrimp and other small sea animals. Narwhals are further north, stay close to ice. Break through with the tusk. Are rarely spotted. Mystery. Mystery becomes myth. A narwhal stays with its mother its whole life—seventy years in the same pod.

76

Deep in the narwhal depths, there are also squid, which gather up their legs and press them back out to swim, which have great black eyes that look like human eyes, which glow ghost-white in the light cast by the deep-sea divers who video them. They gather-push swim away, the squid, squirting black ink in their wake if they've been frightened.

On a lucky day in Maine, you can see dolphins. They leap along the sailboats' sides, riding the wake. Stand on the shore and you will see a whale breach or blow. Puffins sit on rocks, looking startled with their orange beaks. Starting next week, they say we will see the seals sunbathing on the rocks, then slipping back into the water (best of both worlds) and gliding gliding down.

*   *   *

Right

Here we are, back in the top floor of the Arts Building, so close to finishing this year.

They come in talking about their vacations—skiing trips to Vail (my Colorado! I say), and beach trips to Turtle Island and leisurely weeks at the shore house further north or further south. Two of the students who are not from wealth simply went home for the week, to Portland and to Bar Harbor, and the other students say, That's cool. Did you watch a ton of movies? Fun. They are being sincere, but it doesn't come off quite right. It makes me cringe.

I hate Babette, says Ruth. I can't believe I have to see her all the time again. I hate her so much. If you had her as a dorm mother, you'd say it, too, Ms. James.

Mrs. Dregsville, I say.

No—I just spent two hours with her. I earned the right to call her Babette. She's such a bitch. We already had a meeting about keeping the dorm clean for the last month of school. We met at six. This morning. *Six.*

Ruth. You can't curse out other teachers in this class. Zip it.

Fine. I hate Mrs. Dregsville.

But they bring us cake sometimes, says Linda.

Yeah, the banana cake is good.

Linda came in ten minutes late because she was kissing her boyfriend, always kissing her boyfriend. She wrote an essay for class about how in love she is. I am so in love, she wrote. He is my best friend.

Delirious, all of them.

Steven is wearing a suit and his hair is combed. His tie is tied and his shirt is buttoned. Last week, he came in all undone—cuffs and no tie and his hair a mess. Ha ha! Kathryn laughed and pulled a toothbrush and toothpaste out of Steven's pocket.

Today, Steven eats cottage cheese out of a plastic cup with a silver spoon. Kathryn takes the spoon from him. She scoops up the cottage cheese and smears it onto his arm, cackling. She has a wicked cackle—a hard fast laugh that flaunts her wholehearted joy.

Steven laughs. Says, What are you doing? But he doesn't move. Doesn't even flinch.

She laughs harder and smears it on his cheek.

Hey! he says.

Outside, I say. We are going outside.

I stand up. None of them move. They are sloths. They are all talking. Talking sloths. Jabbering sloths.

Why are we going outside? says Linda. It's cold out.

Just for a few minutes, I say.

We're really going? says Iris.

Yes.

Let's go, says Abigail. Come on, everyone.

They move. Maria groans. Steven says, Can I go wash the fluff off my arm?

Fluff? I say.

Yeah, it's fluff.

I thought it was cottage cheese.

Kathryn laughs harder. Linda laughs, too.

We walk up the stairs and out the door. It is cold and dewy.

We walk down the driveway to the old elm trees. They are thirty feet tall and looming, shadows cast on the ground over the green grass. Behind the trees are the soccer and lacrosse and baseball fields. No football team (not enough players). Beyond the fields are the trees, and then the bay.

Well, I say. I don't tell them I thought of this five minutes before class, that I was tucked away with BP all week and let myself forget this place, this class, this school.

This is lame, says Kathryn. She hides behind one of the trees, fifty feet away, hands in her pockets, shoulders hunched up by her ears.

It is lame, I say. Come closer and we'll go in sooner. She runs from one tree to the next, hiding from the wind. She stands beside the group, huddled by the tree. Old tree trunk that's seen the all-male version of this school. Piles and piles of snow. The melting of snow into Spring. The throngs of soccer players on the field. The people on their cell phones, walking. Countless kissing couples. I've found condoms in this field, walking with Andie. Yeah, said My One Friend when I told him last fall, the kids do it out there at night. They sneak out of their dorms.

My One Friend will still not speak to me. He'll wave from afar, but that's all.

It's springtime, I say. So we're going to paint the green and the blooms. Look around. Look at the shadow of the trees on the grass. Look at the buds on the trees and the flowers blooming. Choose any one thing and make a sketch so you can paint it inside. Choose a flower, or the horizon, or a patch of grass. Whatever. One thing.

Can I paint pictures of my vacation? says Iris.

Not right now, I say. Just try this.

Can we go in now? says Steven. It's cold.

Not yet, I say. Just get your sketch, and then we're going to do one more thing.

They dutifully spread out across the field and find their objects. Sketch in their sketchpads.

Okay! shouts Abigail from a bush at the edge of the field. I'm done!

Okay, I say, now draw whatever is in front of or behind your object. Make a five inch square on your page like we did at the beginning of the year, and draw as much detail as you can in that small space.

They all borrow each other's notebooks to make straight lines, and draw the boxes.

Can we go in now? says Steven.

All right, I say, when you're done, you can go in.

They race to the door. On his way, Steven grabs a fistful of grass. He gets inside, to the stairwell that leads back to our classroom, and throws it onto Kathryn's head. She stands there laughing, grass in a pile in her hair, falling onto her shoulders.

I laugh. Great, I say, into the classroom.

Inside, I tell them to make a painting of the three objects they sketched, either together or in three separate pieces. They should use watercolor, the quickest paint.

They sit there and do it. They have accumulated stacks of these things, assignments that I have made up by the seat of my pants. Five minutes left and what will we do? Aha!

Well. I am tired, but I will make up for it. I give plenty of slide shows on the artists they should know, and plenty of reading. Plenty of drawing assignments—*real* ones. Plenty of feedback. I give my time to these fiends.

And I like them. Strange how I like them. How they make me laugh. They are all kinds of tangled up inside, and they struggle and they yearn and they are honest and silly and good.

Next is lunchtime, and I walk to the dining hall. Now that the students are back, and the dining hall is loud again, full of backpacks in the hallway and students bustling in their blazers and khakis and skirts and button-downs and loafers, and the teachers at their three tables in the same attire. I see My One Friend and wave, but he does not wave back. He turns and says something to Jessica, who laughs, her baloney curls bouncing. Talking Man sits beside her eating corn on the cob.

The young faculty are at this table together, the older faculty spread out at the other two tables—except for Leonard, who is like an old man already and wears a golf hat to class every day.

My Devout Roommate comes out of the serving area with her tray in her hands, and I smile and say, Hi, and she does not smile back. She pretends I am invisible. She walks right by. She sits down on the other side of the young faculty table, in the last empty chair, next to Ben and Nicole and Lucy. I turn to the serving area, and walk down the line with my tray and my silverware, and ask for macaroni and cheese, and Mags, the lady who serves it, asks how I am.

I get some chocolate milk and hot chocolate (the best things about the dining hall, that ski-lodge-hot-chocolate machine), and walk to the tables. Right up to the young faculty table. And say, Hi everyone. How was your vacation?

But only Lucy and Nicole smile and say, Good, how was yours? Talking Man says, You're looking well today, Ms. James, and My Devout Roommate scoffs.

What? I say. What did you say, Lexi?

She looks up at me.

Nothing, she says. I didn't say a word.

Right, I say.

I glance up and see Iris and Ruth at the table behind the faculty table, watching us. I smile. They smile, sympathetic. They turn to each other. Ruth takes a bite of her macaroni. Iris eats salad, has been saying she has fat thighs, thoughts I try to talk her out of.

I turn and look for Mr. Griffiths or Mrs. Souci, but don't see them here. I walk to the old-faculty table, and sit down beside Leonard. Talk about his golf game. Handicap. Dates set for play. He asks me if I'd like to go sailing sometime on his family's schooner, and I say, Sure, sounds fun, thanks. I look back at the other table, and see them talking and laughing, and I am in high school again—this place can send me reeling back. I am in high school and the girls are catty and make fun of my height, my pants too short (*waiting for a flood, Anne?* said Jenny Deed in ninth grade), and I have to go to CCD every Sunday night and sit next to the soccer players, who are all rich and who all believe in this religion and themselves, no questions asked, and I do not fit there. I just don't fit.

I go to my mailbox at lunchtime, and sitting in the wooden cubby is a note from the Headmaster. *Dear Ms. James*, it says, *Please make an appointment with my secretary. We need to speak at your earliest convenience.*

That night, I call Gail and say, Shit. I think I'm getting fired. Maybe they heard about the herpes conversation. Or the safe sex talk. Shit. And she says, No, you won't get fired. What could they fire you for? You teach the kids. You spend a lot of time helping them. No way. Can you leave for the whole summer? Why don't you come back to Crested Butte and stay with us? We'd love to have you. You need to get out of there for a bit.

Yeah? I say. I miss the mountains.

Yeah, she says, It'd be so fun.

All right, I say. I could direct the arts camp again. They sent me a letter and want me back.

Hell's bells! she says. Perfect.

So it's a light at the end of the tunnel, an escape hatch waiting.

*   *   *

Sent: April 5, 2004, 2:14pm
To: Anne James
Because it is a fleshly religion and always has been—the body of Christ, the blood of Christ. And because if God wanted women to be priests, he would have sent down a woman. He didn't. He sent a man. So, men's bodies are closer to God than women's. Because of the flesh. They are meant to be the spiritual leaders. And women have other roles in the church. You see?

   Pax et bunum

      -- Talking Man

Sent: April 5, 2004, 2:18pm
To: Talking Man

No. I do not **see.**
      -- Anne

*   *   *

Little Wooden Chair

Come in, says the Headmaster the next day. Have a seat.

He does not gesture to the two couches but to the straight-backed wooden chair between the couches, set there for the troublemakers.

Okay, I say. I sit down on one of the couches instead. I refuse to be a student here.

He clears his throat. His white hair moves from the top of his head as he sits down, his comb-over undone, and then it settles again when he sits.

I asked you to come here, he says, because you know the rule.

Which rule? I say. There are a lot.

He chuckles. Scratches his eyebrow with one finger.

I'm a little uncomfortable speaking about this, he says. He grins a tight grin. Says, The one about overnight guests of the opposite sex.

Oooh, I say. *That rule.* Yes. I laugh. Cross my legs. Think: You have got to be kidding.

Well, I saw that your friend's car was there overnight and in the morning when I woke up, and I had to say something about it or those guys (he gestures to the Abbey) would have my head.

The monks, I say, Of course. They'd surely know if you didn't chastise me.

Well, you know the rules. We made the rules very clear when you moved in. And it's a small school where people notice things.

Of course, I say.

We are both parrots. *Well. Of course.* I hate him. He is my father. I am a teenager. I am in trouble after church. I am in trouble for not doing my homework, for talking back. Always talking back. Always arguing. *Patriarchy, Patriarchy,* running through my head. *And he wanted me to sit in the little wooden chair?*

He's just a friend, I say.

He cocks his head to one side and smirks, as if to say, *Come on.* He says, I saw you holding hands across the soccer field one day.

Oh, you know how cozy friends can be these days, Mr. Swift! I smile and lean forward, playing dumb. I consider slapping his knee with my hand but think better of it.

He clears his throat and starts in again, It's simply not permitted, Ms. James. We would hate for the students to see such an example set, you know? We're all here for the students' sake; I say this to you with *their* best interest at heart....

He keeps talking, but I am not listening. I watch the students through the curtain-framed window behind him. I tune in when he says, So, that's all. Just don't do it again, please, or we'll have to take further action.

Further action, I say.

Right, he says.

Just one question, I say. I raise one hand. I feel my face is red. I feel the anger rising up like it used to when I was told I could not do one thing or another, that my brother Ed could stay out till ten but I had to be home by eight—different rules for girls, different dangers.

Sure, he says, shoot. He's leaning forward on the other couch, his navy blazer open. Pinstriped shirt and shiny red tie.

How did you see his car? Our cottage is tucked away in the trees. How could you have possibly seen his car?

He turns and looks out the window, where the students walk between classes in their summer attire, short-sleeved and in skirts with sandals, partially liberated, and a monk walks by in his robes, and two teachers chat side by side.

He looks back at me.

I just noticed, he said.

There is a long pause.

Someone told you, I say. Didn't they?

He shakes his head. No, he says, Nope, no one told me. Mr. O'Malley did say you were in the Admin Building playing the piano, which is fine—we encourage you to use the facilities here. But no one told me he'd stayed over.

Your house is a mile away, on the other side of campus.

Ms. James, he says, I think we're finished here. So long as we're clear about the future. Yes?

I don't say anything back. I give him a look and shake my head and purse my lips, beyond angry, afraid of what I'll say, and I walk out of his office. Silent.

*   *   *

The Rule of St. Benedict (Prologue)
"Seeking his workman in a multitude of people, the Lord calls out to him and lifts his voice again: 'Is there anyone here who yearns for life and desires to see good days?' (Ps 33[34]:13). If you hear this and you answer is, 'I do,' God then directs these words to you: 'If you desire true and eternal life, keep your tongue free from vicious talk and your lips from all deceit; turn away from evil and do good; let peace be your quest and aim' (Ps 33[34]:14-15). Once you have done this 'my eyes will be upon you and my ears will listen for your prayers; and even before you ask me, I will say to you: Here I am' (Isa 58:9). What, dear brothers, is more delightful than this voice of the Lord calling to us? See how the Lord in his love shows us the way of life. Clothed then with faith and the performance of good works, let us set out on this way, with the Gospel for our guide, that we may deserve to see him 'who has called us to his kingdom' (1 Thess 2:12)" (Fry 16)

*   *   *

Indoctrinate: Both my parents came from Catholic families, my mother French, my father Irish. Rosaries spun into my grandparents' hands. Church every Sunday. A check for the basket. They grew up with Mass in Latin. Catholic school. Nuns to slap your hands with rulers. *You have no idea,* say my parents, *what those nuns were like. They were tough cookies.* When I told my grandfather, in college, that I was a vegetarian, he said, *You're too nice a girl to be a vegetarian.* Nice girls are sweet and don't talk back and keep their hair long and go to church on Sundays and are not easy (my mother's word) and eat meat.

*   *   *

That Night

Well, says my mother over the phone, you knew the rules. They did tell you.

Get out of there! says Gail. It's making you sad! It isn't worth it.

My brother laughs. I can't believe you got in trouble for it, he says. Oh my God, that's funny.

I call BP and leave him a message. He isn't home from work yet. He won't be home until six.

When Lexi comes home at five, after soccer practice (assistant coach), she jogs up to her room in her cleats, leaving dirt clods all in her trail, and closes the door. I go up and knock.

Lexi, I say, open up. I need to talk to you.

There is a pause, silence. Andie comes up and sits on my feet. Watches the door.

Lexi, I say.

The door opens. She sits on the edge of her bed in her sweatpants and an oversized t-shirt that comes to her knees.

What's going on? I say. Why is no one talking to me? And how did the Headmaster know about BP?

I don't know, she says.

Well, then, why aren't *you* talking to me?

What do you call this? she says.

I lean on the doorframe and sigh. Cross my arms. Andie goes into the room and wags her tail at Lexi. Sits at her feet. Waits to be petted. Lexi doesn't like her. Cringes when Andie leans against her legs. Says, Uch, that dog sheds like crazy. But she wanted the free rent, so she agreed to it.

I want to call Andie away, tell her not to be so nice.

Look, I say, I would never tell anyone about you and Jessica. I've been looking for you the last week to tell you that, but you haven't been around. I don't care what you do. It's fine with me. I'm happy for you, actually. And if you don't want anyone to know, you don't have to worry about me saying anything. BP didn't even see. It was only me. I swear, my lips are sealed.

She looks at me. She is blushing. Her hair is sweaty and pulled back in a ponytail.

I don't know what you're talking about, she says.

Really? I say.

Really, she says.

Come on, Lexi, I say, stop pretending. It's okay. You don't have to hide.

She shakes her head. There's nothing to hide, she says, because nothing's happening. She looks at me and her eyes are cold, as if she's detached from now. She's somewhere else, retreating.

I'm *okay* with it, Lexi. You don't have to hide.

I'm not hiding anything. You, on the other hand, broke the rule.

I stare at her. A long minute.

You told, didn't you? It was you.

She shakes her head and looks at her knees, pulls the shirt lower.

No, she says.

Then how on earth did Mr. Swift know?

Maybe Mr. L told.

No way, I say. He'd never. Then I think: Would he? Would he do that now?

She sighs, the kind that catches in the throat. She says, I was only trying to help you, if you won't save yourself. When she looks up at me, I see her eyes welling up, that she's near tears. Why would she do this when she has her own secret, when she's seeing Jessica?

You hypocrite, I say, and turn and walk downstairs, pull on my sneakers and call Andie. Walk down to the shore and walk and walk and walk, stumbling over the rocks, until sunset, and then past sunset, until it is dark and I am calm again and the water is black and almost quiet and the sky is moonless. The lighthouse across the bay spins an arc of light across the water, almost touches us, spins on.

We will drive to BP's house for the night. We will sleep there, and come back in the morning. I turn and walk the rocky shoreline back, an hour and a half in the dark, pine trees dark silhouettes above me, above the boulders on the shoreline, Andie's collar jingling ahead, leading the way home.

*　　　*　　　*

Sent: April 8, 2004
To: St. Christopher's Faculty and Staff
Thanks to everyone who helped me find Sadie this afternoon. She
was at the science building construction site, looking for bones. Ha
ha. Mr. Jones found her on his way to the dining hall. She's home
safe and sound now. Thanks again.

       --   *Nicole Holt*

          *   *   *

Late night TV: Mel Brooks is dressed up as a nun, dancing. A
whole row of nuns dancing, and then the priests, and they jump
into a pool of water, and it is something ridiculous and hilarious.

          *   *   *

Wound

The next night, Steven says, Ms. James, my leg is bleeding. I
looked down and it was bleeding.

What happened? I say. It is intermission at the play, *West Side
Story*. A scaffolding and singing and dance routines—very elab-
orate for a high school play, the works. I am talking to two other
teachers, two of three who will speak to me now, Mr. West and
Nicole. He pulled me aside just before the play began and told me
that Lexi has been telling people that I am a sinner, that I drink at
night alone and go to class drunk sometimes, too. Why? I asked
him, and he shrugged and said he didn't know. I see Mr. West
every day when I walk into my classroom. We teach across from
one another. He knows I am no drunk. He says he'll vouch for me.
So this is why everyone's shutting me out? I say. He nods. Yeah, he
says. But we don't believe it. He means him and Nicole and Lucy.
He says, Mr. L stood up for you, too. He told everyone that was
ridiculous, that you'd never do that.

Steven says, I kicked the chair and there was a spiky thing sticking out of it, and I went to the bathroom and it was bleeding.

He interrupts to tell me of his trials.

I say, A spiky thing?

Yeah, a metal thing, on the chair, he says.

He pulls up the back of his pants leg and shows me. A narrow sliver of skin shaved off. A tiny circle of blood. He touches it with one finger, says, See? Bleeding.

He leans against the pole beside him. As if he is weakened.

Mr. West and Nicole lean forward to look, then turn to each other and roll their eyes.

Maybe you need a Band-Aid, I say. It looks like you're going to live.

I put toilet paper on it, he says. In the bathroom.

That's good. Go put some more on there. Stick it in the back of your shoe.

He nods. He turns and begins to wander off.

See you Monday, Steven.

He nods and walks away.

Maybe she is saying it so that if I tell about her and Jessica, no one will believe me. They will think I'm an unreliable source. A drunk is always a liar, they will think. Maybe this is why. Every night since our talk, I have stayed with BP in Portland. Driven down each night and up each morning.

In the opening act, there is Mr. L, one of four special invited faculty performers. He plays a cop, very tall, and writes down the students' misdeeds. And now they sing and play wild, singing, *Sick! Sick! We're sick in the head!* And falling in love, and fighting with each other. They strut and chew gum and pretend to be hardened. They look so young.

Sit down, says Nicole beside me. She pats the empty seat. She and Mr. West are laughing laughing hard. Mr. West unbuttons his jacket (dress code, you must attend the play in dress code).

How could you not bend over laughing at Steven? they say. That was hilarious.

They are really laughing hard.

You were so caring and compassionate with him, and asking what happened; I would have laughed in his face!

Oh, I say. He has some dramatic thing every day. One day, he laid back on my desk and said he thought he was dying.

I think: Every day this week, in fact, he has mentioned that someone will die, or he hopes he doesn't die, or he wants to kill so and so for doing such and such. Death on the brain. I've laughed it away, but maybe I should not.

He's one of my favorites, I say. He's funny.

He must know that, says one of them, because he came up to tell you about his blister and interrupted our conversation for it.

Yeah, I say. They all have these tremendous problems. Like, *My roommate rearranged my room!*

What I don't say is how I understand, and how each small problem is just a symbol of their bigger, teenage angst.

They love you, says the other. Abigail's in your class, right? She loves you. She tells me during our house meetings.

Oh, I say, thanks.

In this high school, the other teachers laugh and commiserate and make fun. But I feel sorry for Steven, so far from his mother. I know he is homesick. Know he is only sixteen, and thousands of miles from home. *Sweden*, he writes every week in one assignment or another, *I miss you, Sweden.* I know this feeling. I know what it is to miss a place. I think of Crested Butte. I think of the mountains. That longing.

When I walk away, they laugh about something else, shoulders pressed together.

At the end of the play, a boy is murdered. A fight over a girl and then he dies. The crowd is very very quiet. The boy lies back on his girlfriend's lap, and she weeps and moans. She is good, this actress, with a voice that rises up above everyone else's. And when they sing with her, they sing better, too.

All the students in the audience are very, very quiet as she weeps. They have catcalled and howled during the stage-kisses and the songs, but now there is a hush, in this darkness. What are they thinking now? What are they thinking as she weeps?

The lights come up and everyone cheers. The teachers who acted in the play come out first and the crowd roars for them. They bow and smile. And then the students, in rows—in their fifties dresses, their fifties jeans, their tank tops and their coral flouncy skirts with button-downs tied up in knots.

Time to go, everyone flows out. The young faculty will go out and eat dinner together. They'll all go out drinking, Lexi tagging along with Jessica behind her. I notice she does not speak much to Jessica now, that Jessica is being left out, too. And I am not part of the group at all, now that Mr. L's stopped talking to me and Lexi's spreading rumors. Which is fine—better, really.

I think of my sophomore year in high school, when my best friend was at a house party, and me and two other friends knocked on the door and were told we weren't allowed; there's not enough room, they said. We wondered why our friend, inside, wouldn't vouch for us, and how she was chosen but we were not. Those faraway past times should not exist in me anymore. But they do. They still do.

I walk faster and catch up to Lexi in the foyer. Hey, I say, Lexi. I grab her elbow. She turns. Scowls.

What? she says.

I need to talk to you for a minute.

She rolls her eyes. You and your conversations, she says.

Now, I say. Unless you want me to talk right here, in front of everyone. I raise my eyebrows, blackmailing her.

Bye, Ms. James, says Steven, behind me. Bye, say Linda and Ruth.

Bye, I say. I turn and smile and wave. I see Brother Timothy at the far end of the room and he catches my eye, and I wave to him, too.

Lexi and I walk to the door, push it open, walk outside. Stand in the middle of the green wet lawn while everyone walks to their cars.

What? she says. She throws up her hands.

Don't give me that, I say, You know what. Telling people I'm a *drunk*? Are you insane? Are you trying to get me fired?

She looks away. Crosses her arms. Says, Please. You're talking crazy again.

No, Lexi. Mr. West told me what you've been saying. You'd better fix it or I will get you in so much trouble. I'll tell about you and Jessica, too. I will.

She rolls her eyes and walks away.

I'm serious, I say to her back.

I stand there for a minute, catching my breath, listening to the murmurs as everyone leaves, the sighs of *it was so good, and Henry's face, oh my God, and that was such a funny line, I can't believe he kissed her.*

I walk to the path and join them, and as the crowd moves out, I hustle away, pretending I am doing something Very Important, which will take up my whole evening and make me deliciously happy. I am wanted! my walk says. Can't you see? Going *someplace*! Where people are waiting for me! That group is going out drinking. But I'll go home and paint, a delicious night in the quiet house. I'll see BP tomorrow. I want to drive straight home and work all night.

Someone hollers, Anne! when I am almost at the path across the field, the shortcut through the woods to our cottage, and I turn and see Mr. L, running toward me.

Hey, he says.

Hi, I say.

He stands in front of me for a moment, breathless.

I say, You're talking to me again?

I know. I'm sorry. He shakes his head, hands on his hips. He looks at the ground.

It's been lonely, I say.

He nods. It was just because–, he says.

But I stop him. I know, I say. I wasn't very nice, either. I called you to apologize, a bunch of times.

Sorry, he says again.

Thanks for sticking up for me.

Of course, he says. She's being ridiculous.

And then his students run up behind him shouting, and hug him, and someone pours a bottle of Gatorade on his head as if this was a game, and he shouts and laughs, and they pull him back to school.

Come out with us tonight! he says as he goes, his hair pressed flat against his head.

Some other night, I say. I can't tonight.

And then he's gone inside.

Earlier this week, in class after the lunch incident, Ruth said, Ms. James, do you hang out with the other women teachers?

Not really, I said, Well, sometimes.

They're so cliquey, she said. Ms. Swenson and Ms. Dinse. They're not nice.

Oh, they're fine, I said. They're nice. Let's talk about it *after* class. Let's not gossip now.

Okay, they said.

I don't know why I felt I had to protect everyone else, to not let the students in on the truth. How many times have they asked if I like living with Ms. Dinse? And I always say, Yes.

But the students notice everything. They see it all.

*   *   *

"...[L]et us ask the Lord...: 'Who will dwell in your tent, Lord; who will find rest upon your holy mountain?' (Ps 14[15]:1). After this question, brothers, let us listen well to what the Lord says in reply... 'One who walks without blemish,' he says, 'and is just in all his dealings; who speaks the truth from his heart and has not practiced deceit with his tongue...' (Ps 14[15]:2-3)." (Fry 17-18).

*   *   *

My mother says her Jewish friend Trudy couldn't sell her apartment. This was in New York, and my mother had flown out for a visit. She hates to fly but she goes to see her college roommates every year. So, Trudy could not sell her apartment, and my mother told her about St. Joseph. We have to go to church, said Trudy. Saint Patrick's is right down the street. I told her fine, we'll say a prayer. So we went into the cathedral, says my mother, and Trudy walks right up front and lights a candle! My mother laughs. I wasn't sure about this. But then we kneeled down and said a prayer. I told her to buy the statue, too, says my mother. She couldn't find one so I sent one to her. I guess she can't bury it in the ground, so she set it on her porch. So, I get home and three days later, her apartment's sold. Your father's boss tried it, too, and he sold his house two days after he lit the candle. How about *that*, she says.

*   *   *

By Email

The next morning, very early, Lexi is crying at the dining room table, head in her arms. I stand at the top of the stairs and look down at her.

I walk down the five steps. Pull a chair out and sit at the table, across from her.

She raises her head and looks at me. Her eyes are mooned in red. Her cheeks are puffed and taut.

She sees me and says, I'm sorry. I'm really sorry. I shouldn't have done that, about the Headmaster and BP. I shouldn't have told.

She is still wearing that big t-shirt, her hair flat and sweaty.

Lexi, I say, it's okay. I'll forgive you, okay? And I'm still not going to say anything about you and Jessica. I never was.

She shakes her head. Catches her breath.

I'll tell everyone, she says, I'll tell them I made it up.

Okay, I say. Today? You'll talk to the Headmaster, everyone?

Yeah, she says, Yes.

Why'd you do it?

She shrugs. Sniffs. Looks out the window. The ocean is roaring today. The wind whipping around the house. She looks into her hands, and says almost in a whisper, In case. In case you told.

I nod. That's what I thought, I say.

She keeps crying. I sit there and wait it out. I don't feel big enough to hug her, to comfort her.

Then she looks up. There's bad news, she says. We got an email.

What? I say. I think of Steven, his dramatic acts, his cut, how I should have talked to the Psychiatrist about him, how he's been talking about death so much lately.

What? I say again.

Mr. L, she says, was in a car accident in town last night.

In Portland?

She nods. My heart skips.

But he's okay, I say.

She shakes her head. He's in the hospital. In a coma. He was drunk. Mr. West was with him, but he's fine. Just a broken arm and some bruises.

Shit, I say. Oh, God.

I run to the bathroom and throw up.

They sent out an email, she says when I come back. You don't look so good. Are you okay? Can you believe they'd say that in an email?

I shake my head, stunned.

We didn't know he was driving home. He just took off, disappeared, and we thought for a while he was in the bathroom. But then he never showed up again. And then this morning—oh, God, she says. And cries again, and I think of him last night with his hair wet, laughing as the students pulled him back to school, how I was relieved that we'd be friends again, not angry anymore, just happy. How he kissed me on the wall that day, and then that long stupid silence. And then I begin to cry, and Lexi stands up and hugs me. Doesn't say anything about praying, or God, or Jesus—no lessons. Just hugs me.

Later that morning, I go to Dr. Pell's office and talk to her about Steven. Say, I am worried, and she nods in her owl glasses and takes notes and says she'll call him in.

Long-faced

All the students are forlorn. Lackluster. Stunned. They love Mr. L. And now he is on the brink, teetering. For three days, we have waited, unsure. There are extra Masses. There are prayers. Brother Timothy leads the students through a prayer at the assembly. For Mr. L to heal, for Mr. West to heal, for all of us to stay strong and united. Some of the students are angry. *We always hear 'don't drink and drive,' and then he goes and does it? What an idiot. What a jerk. We don't even do that.* Some are just sad. Some laugh in shared moments, and then look up with guilt in their faces, as if they should not be laughing. It's okay to laugh, says the faculty, you should laugh sometimes. It's okay to live.

(The faculty is stunned, too. But for them, for the students, we say that this will soon start to hurt less. There will be better times up ahead for us. And he will make it, and we will make it, all of us, if we stay together now.)

The students take their sketchpads to the stone boathouse. I take out the acrylics and we look at Rothkos and make abstractions. They paint watercolors with portable paint sets, sitting in the sunshine in the field that faces the bay, that wide sloping field. There are steps set into the hill, where Steven and Kathryn sit side by side. No shenanigans this week. The others flop onto the grass. Iris falls asleep on her stomach, brush in hand, and I let her sleep until class is over. They are the same as ever, but bruised. Tender at the edges. Quieter. They are afraid.

I look out at the ocean and imagine its creatures swimming underneath, ignorant of our world: the whales, the narwhals, the glow-white squid and their human staring eyes. Swimming in darkness unless someone with a flashlight comes along.

There was a special Mass this morning, and I went. Walked into the church. Did not recite the *Our Father* or the *Hail Mary*. Did not cross myself when that time came, did not go up for Communion (the Headmaster glanced my way from his perch in the balcony), but I was there. For my students. For Mr. L and Mr. West. I prayed, not to their version of God but my own.

Brother Matthew said a prayer, and everyone bowed their heads and was very quiet. The sound of a creaking pew. The sound of a boy clearing his throat. The sound of our breath coming in and going out. I envied all those people who can bow their heads, and let go, saying: It is in God's hands now. I envied them that faith, the belief that whatever happens to Mr. L is what is meant to happen, that we will accept his living or his dying as God's will. I can't practice that sort of surrender. When I prayed, it was to keep him here.

This afternoon, the students walk out saying, Happy weekend. Happy Friday. I want to stop them—Iris, Steven, Ruth—and suspend the rest of our lives to keep them here, tell them stories, paint together, all weekend, into each night. *We'll huddle together,* I'll tell them, *you are safe.* I want to protect them from this pain, to shield them should he die—to stop them from entering the world at all, where there's too much danger.

*   *   *

On the radio, a historian says: Because he gave the people so much hope, their hearts were broken when he was crucified.

Knowing something is against the odds, and believing in it anyway.

*   *   *

Brother Slabs

Up at school, at the corner where the second driveway leads along the bay and then winds into all the buildings, just at that entrance, there is a graveyard with three rows of old stone grave markers. These are the graves of the priests and the monks who have died. There was a funeral this winter, a monk who had been in the hospital over a year. One more marker added.

This gravesite is strange, just at the entrance to the school. A good omen? Spirits watching over us? A warning of what might come? A reminder to live a good life?

I don't notice it unless I am looking, on a walk with Andie, perhaps, on my way to get coffee. On my way to the hockey rink, where my students played hockey this winter, and turned red-cheeked on Sunday afternoons.

I try not to let Andie into the graveyard because it seems disrespectful. I try to keep her on the road.

Today, I walk past the graveyard, and then down to the bay, and stand on the rocky beach, and look out at the flat span of water. Mr. Griffiths walks Rufus and turns back, sees me, waves, and then walks on. I smell the salty smell again. I rock back and forth over the stones, picking slowly, sun sinking down all thick and yellow, wind on my face. I pick up a flat stone and try to skip it like BP did. It lands and sinks in one spot. The wind picks up. Always, the wind.

*   *   *

At the Sistine Chapel in Rome, we walk through and look up. This is during college, after I've given up church but before the pedophile news emerged. There is a crowd around us. We are very young—only twenty—and very lucky. Three of us come to see the Sistine Chapel. We take a tour of the whole Vatican, home of the Pope, where he has lived for hundreds and hundreds of years. The same hunched white man in long draping robes. The same red beanie on his head (there must be a name for it—I don't know). The same squinting eyes looking out upon the crowd. The same slow wave, a raised hand, an old man.

The Pope has been there forever and ever. Amen.

Sometimes I think in blasphemies.

At the end of the tour, we walk through a chapel. And one of the girls, who is not Catholic, says, The Catholic church is so strange. It's done so many terrible things. It's so rich—look at all of this. All of this for the Pope! It's ridiculous.

I agree with her, entirely. But she is not Catholic. It's like calling someone else's mother a pain in the ass.

The Pope is in charge of all of this, she says, and he's so out of touch with the world. He's like a cult leader, basically.

What do you know about the Catholic church, I say. Have you ever even been to a Mass?

Once, she says. They did that weird communion thing, where you're eating *the body of Christ*. Come on, she says.

That's what Catholics believe, I say. You don't know anything about it. So you shouldn't really say. He's not a cult leader. It's *tradition*.

I don't think so. He completely oppresses everyone in the church. He makes rules about all this other stuff he has nothing to do with—abortion, birth control. Who does he think he is? It's none of his business.

You don't know what you're talking about, I say. You don't know the first thing about it.

The other girl, who knows me better than the first, says, You don't even like Catholicism, Anne. You haven't been to church in years.

That's beside the point, I say. *She* has no right to criticize. She doesn't know what she's talking about.

I stormed out of the chapel in a fury, and I wouldn't talk to the first girl until well into our pizza lunch at a little café down the road, where everything was too expensive because of all the tourists. A trap. We paid our fee to walk through the Vatican. It was true—all of that wealth, for the Pope, for a church. The place must be priceless. A ceiling painted by Michelangelo? Whose skin came off with his boots when he finally removed them because of all the sweat? Was that commissioned in honor of God, or was that simply greed, vanity? *If we look powerful, if we have all of this, we must be right…*

There was a time the church collected money to send lost souls to Heaven. As if the money given here would be sent to God up there.

Religion does not make sense to me. Religion does not sit well in my body.

God: yes. Most of the time, I think yes. And the stories, I love. But they are just stories.

All the money to build a church, when you might just as well walk up a mountain, to the treeline where the earth turns to rock and the snow is gathered in piles, and the wind picks up and you can look back and see the tops of the trees for miles, a town spread below. What's a gilded room to that? What's a priceless painting?

Now, I would not defend the church. I would agree with that friend.

But this Catholic past is part of me. I can't slice it away. Alright. Even though I do not believe it anymore.

Ex-Catholic. Lapsed Catholic. Recovering Catholic.

Pieces I carry with me.

*   *   *

Revive

Another email tells us Mr. L woke up, he'll be alright, and I drive down that night to see him.

You made it! I say. And he raises his hands above his hand, very slowly, and says, Hoorah! in a small voice.

I brought you flowers, I say, and give him a bunch of pink tulips in a glass vase. Set them on the table beside his bed.

My mom will be back in a minute, he says. His voice sounds all stuffed up. His nose looks broken. He says, She loves tulips.

You look really good, I say.

His cheeks are all puffed, dark circles under his eyes and a bruise down the right side of his head, all purple and brown and yellow.

No, I don't, he says.

We laugh a little.

But you're okay? I say, and he says yes, and then I hold his hand and sit until his mother comes in, bustling, with a plastic bag full of sandwiches. Three different kinds, because she wasn't sure what Andrew would like.

Andrew introduces us. Mrs. LeGarde.

What lovely flowers, she says. She goes into the bathroom with a plastic cup, fills it with water, and arranges the flowers on Andrew's table. She has short red hair, and wears glasses, too, like Andrew.

I feel so stupid, he says. What's happening with the kids?

Same old, same old, I say.

He nods.

But, he says, they know?

His mother opens up the plastic bag, unwraps the chicken salad, the ham, the turkey with Swiss. Sets them on their wrappers on the tray that swings over Andrew's bed.

Yeah, I say. Some of them are pretty mad at you.

He nods. He picks up the ham sandwich and stares at it a minute.

Sweetheart? says his mother. She takes one step toward his bed.

He looks up, looks at me. He says, I think that place is toxic.

That night, I go to the coffee shop and find BP, who sits in back with his laptop, working. He smiles when he sees me. I sit down beside him.

Andrew's back, I say.

Good, he says, Oh, good.

Yes, I say.

And then we go to his house, and sit down on the couch, and Green lies on our feet, and we just rest a while.

Brother Timothy

Says he has two daughters, says he wishes his daughters would visit more, says they do not understand this choice, to live here, to become a monk. Says, They wish I hadn't chosen to stay here forever, because that's what being a Benedictine Monk *is*, a commitment to this single place. I have to get permission from the Abbott to leave. To go to the doctor, to go to the dentist. Says, I love silence. When I went to the dentist last week, I didn't play the radio in the car, because I loved to have that silence. The world now, it's all crowded with noise. Students are always listening to their iPods and watching TV. Oh, it's too much, he says. A place changes the longer you stay in it, you know. They aren't just the same trails every day; the plants change—they grow or die—and sometimes there are rabbits, when it's wet there are frogs, in summer—cicadas. I imagine being here, in this one place, is like being in a long marriage, and the way you shift and mold to one another as time goes on. A *good* marriage, I mean. He shakes his head. Mine wasn't good. You probably heard what happened to my wife. He glances at me, and I nod. His wife was committed, years ago, and cannot speak anymore. He turns to the milk machine in the cafeteria, and fills his glass. It froths up white. He says, Let's sit and talk about books, all right? All right, I say, and we walk to a table by ourselves, at the far end of the dining hall, and talk for half an hour before he has to go back to pray.

Homework

They don't do it anymore, the homework. Mr. L and Mr. West's accident has set them off-track, and summer is coming, and now, they do nothing. Come to class and lean back in their chairs, put their Ugg boots up in front of them. Relax.

For two weeks, I was patient, but then came word that Mr. L would be all right, had woken up and was just the same as ever. And Mr. West walks around campus waving to everyone, talking talking, and I am losing my patience with them now. And I am worried. If I want to leave, I have to have money from someplace. Money enough to move. Another job somewhere. I cannot stand another year, I think, but where else can I go? Back to Crested Butte? Find something there? What will give me time to paint? This place is not worth the time. It isn't.

Sometimes I wonder if they are a generation of do-nothings, spoiled, passive, without inspiration. *We can't do anything about the problems. What can we do? The world is melting. Big diff.* Only they don't say "big diff." Big diff is a phrase from my generation. A phrase these kids would never ever use.

We're doing a unit on the 60s, so all week, we look at art by Andy Warhol, Ellsworth Kelly, Alice Neel, Elizabeth Catlett. We listen to the Beatles and talk about the assassinations of JFK and Martin Luther King, Jr. Later, we'll listen to Woody Guthrie, The Doors, The Jackson Five, Janis Joplin, and Aretha Franklin while we paint. But first, I have them read "A & P" for homework, classic story of a teenage boy. *He's so dramatic*, they say. *He thinks quitting his job is the end of the world and it isn't. He's just a typical teenager.*

Yeah, they say. Yeah yeah yeah. Like a bunch of beatniks. Beatniks with Chanel earrings and Scoop pants and two hundred dollar blazers that they stuff into their bags because they hate to wear them.

Well. I don't blame them. I hate blazers, too.

It's just a grocery store job, says Penelope, she of the Coco Chanel diamond earrings. *It's not like it's his life. He hasn't really ruined his life at all. He can go and get a better job than that.*

Can he? I say. What does the grocery store job mean to him?

He thinks it's everything and it's not, they say. *Maybe,* says one of them, *if we knew if it was just summer money or whatever, then it would mean more.*

What do we know about the job and the town? I say. Is there a bounty of opportunity here? Is he well-off?

They shrug.

What does he mean when he says it will affect him for the rest of his life?

That's where he's just being dramatic.

Okay, I say.

Then we close the story. They have so much and care so little. Here they are in their posh world with their posh clothes. Sprawled out before me, one of them falling asleep even, doing nothing. And when I say, No, Steven cannot take the quiz. He said he didn't read the story and then walked out of the room, they all whine and say it will only take a minute, let him let him, then I pull one of their tricks. I roll my eyes. Let him take the quiz after our discussion? No.

Take out a piece of paper, I say, and sketch, in as much detail as possible, a scene at one of your jobs. Five minutes. Go.

I'm spoiled, says Kathryn, *I've never had a job.*

Well, then, I say, draw what you do for school.

I did community service once, does that count?

Yeah, that's perfect, I say. Great.

At the end of class, Ruth says, *Why did you have us do that? We aren't even going to do anything with it?*

It's to help you generate your next painting, I say. Next week, we're using oils. So you can paint the scene of your work. Using details, like Updike did in his story.

Oh, she says. She folds over one corner of her sketch.

The bell rings and they all slouch out the door, feet scuffing over the carpet. Pick up your feet! Pick up your goddamned feet! I scream it at them. I wave my hands in the air like a crazy baboon. I holler and show them my red ass. I hoot and grunt. Tear off all my clothes and dance up on the table. *You you you!* I scream. Get it *together!* Why don't you *care?*

They slouch right out the door, noticing nothing.

Check-in

Brother Matthew comes up to my classroom, where I sit in one of the little chair-desks and stare out at the sea. Overcast, the sun is starting to come through. Shines in little glints on the waves. A sailboat glides by. Seagulls dip above the water, crying. All fall, I'd look out the window to see if someone was hurt out there, moaning, and then realize: Oh, it's the seagull call. Are you okay? he says. Everything okay? Yes, I say, thanks. He sits down in one of the little desks beside me, gathers up his robes so he's not sitting on them. Want some company? he says. Yes, I say. I look at him and then keep watching the bay. And then he tells me a story, how when he was younger it was very hard to make ends meet, but he always did. He just kept his faith in himself and in his work, and he made it just fine. How he was very happy then, even when he was just scraping by. Lived on a pittance, he says, peanut butter and jelly every day for lunch and beans for dinner. Slept on friend's couches. And look at me, he says, I am all right. He smiles, then he laughs and looks out the window. Look at that water, he says, Have you ever seen anything so beautiful?

✳　　✳　　✳

The St. Christopher Herald
Written and published by the students of St. Christopher's Second-
ary School
Pawtucksey, Maine
Advisor: Mary Beth Souci

Overworked Students Face Finals
> *How will students get through finals this week? Turn to p. 10*
> *to find out.*
Will St. Bernard's Win the St. Chris Cup?
> *With a ten point lead, Chris Harkins interviews dorm residents*
> *to learn their secrets, and does some quick math to calculate re-*
> *maining challenges and other dorms' chances at this year's cup.*
St. Christopher Sailing Team Places First in New England Regional
Race
> *Third year running, Captain James Washing reports.*
Student-Nominated Faculty Awards!
> *Mr. L wins Best Teacher. Mr. West wins Most Challenging. Mr.*
> *Jones wins Riotous Stalwart. Ms. Strauss wins Best First Year*
> *Teacher.*
Volunteers Return from New Orleans with Callouses and Stories.
> *While most of us basked in the sunshine, ten student volun-*
> *teers, led by Brother Timothy and Mrs. Still, traveled to New*
> *Orleans for their Spring Break, to work for Habitat for Hu-*
> *manity.*
Opinion: The Dining Hall Needs More Vegan Options, by Kate Bay-
berry.

*   *   *

My mother says that she is going back to the church. It is something she needs, she says. Because she is getting old, says Ed. It
was Thanksgiving when she decided this. We were all there. I
was still with Danny, and he sat in the living room and watched
football with my father while Ed and my mother and I sat at the
island in the kitchen, eating olives and crackers and cheese. I can't
believe you'd go back, I said then. You hate how they treat women.
You think those priests are sick. Well, she said. I need the rit-
ual. It's what I know. I'm getting old, it's true. I have to believe

in something. I go to church and pray now and feel better. And the prayers come true! I prayed that Danny would propose, and look! She pointed to the ring on my finger. I rolled my eyes and smiled. It's like meditating, said Ed. Why don't you go to yoga? I said. She laughed. I need this, she said. I light candles for you, too, you know.

I could have said, I miss the routine, too, sometimes. Reciting those prayers. Sitting, kneeling, standing, shaking hands and saying, *Peace be with you.* Rhythms the body remembers, words I could recite in my sleep.

*   *   *

Revived

Mr. West and I have coffee, lunch, and dinner every day for five days straight. BP is busy in Portland this week, this pro bono case he took on, housing-something-something, but he'll be up on Friday, he says. Okay. So I make do with Talking Man. Mr. West. Jacob. It is good to be friends again.

We can't talk about the rhythm method, I say, or sex. Or religion.

Okay, he says, sure.

What does that leave? I say.

School, he says.

His black eye is fading. Now it is yellow and brown. His arm is still in a sling, in a cast, which he will wear for another month. It's been almost two weeks since the crash. That's what he calls it, *The Great Unfortunate Crash of 2004.* All bravado.

He holds onto the handle when I drive, though, clenching on the turns. They were hit when Mr. L, when Andrew, turned right.

We drive to the little coffee shop in town. Town is a strip of four stores and a diner and a coffee shop. The coffee shop is more like a hut, really, with a curved ceiling, and two tables and six chairs.

Mr. West, Jacob, wears a purple sweater vest and a lime green shirt. Very stylish, I say, and nod to his sweater.

Yeah, he says, I like to keep it on the up and up. He laughs. I'd make a good gay guy, huh? he says. That's what everyone tells me.

I laugh. You would, I say.

Andrew got moved to the regular ward this morning, he says. So we can visit.

Great, I say. I'll go to Portland on Friday, then, instead of having BP come up here.

What's the BP stand for?

He hates it, I say, the real name.

You can't tell me? Jacob scratches his chin. He's growing a beard, and it's coming in scruffy. He can grow a beard because summer is coming, and he's injured. They won't say anything about it.

Well. All right. It's Bartholomew Peterkin. Last name Barnum.

Ohhh, he groans. That's tough.

I take a sip of coffee. He laughs, and I laugh. I say, That's what he thinks, too, I guess.

Is he related to Barnum and Bailey?

No, I say. I laugh. Actually, I don't know. I never asked.

They're from around here, you know. He could be. Circus riches in your future! Jacob puts his hands up by his face and wiggles his fingers, stardust falling on us.

We drive back to campus, and he asks about Lexi.

She's really tight with Jessica, huh?

Oh, I say, I guess. I don't really know.

I focus on the road, both hands on the wheel. Avoiding the big holes in the dirt. A squirrel runs out in front of the car and I stop short.

Jesus! screams Jacob. Jesus Christ! He puts both hands on the dashboard to stop himself from going through the window.

He leans forward. Purple sweater vest. Back heaving. Blonde head in his hands.

Are you okay? I say. I'm sorry, it was just a squirrel. I hit the brake too hard. Are you all right?

I touch his back. Rub up and down.

Yeah, he says. I'm fine.

He sits up again, his face flushed. Leans back in the seat. Puts his hand up on the handle loop on the ceiling.

I'm fine, he says. Go ahead.

It's hard to shake these things, I say.

Yeah. I didn't think I was that scared.

I know.

And then I ease the car into gear again, and roll slowly forward, inching the rest of the way home. It takes ten minutes this way, and we are both late for class. But it does not really matter. We are very nearly done.

*   *   *

"...Never swerving from his instructions, then, but faithfully observing his teaching in the monastery until death, we shall through patience share in the sufferings of Christ that we may deserve also to share in his kingdom. Amen (Prologue, Fry, 18).

> *"[Here begins the text of the rule]*
> *[It is called a rule because it regulates*
> *the lives of those who obey it]*

Chapter 1. The Kinds of Monks
There are clearly four kinds of monks..."

(Fry 20)

*   *   *

Abort

Two weeks later, there is one week left of school, and Jacob West is not my friend anymore. A turned back, his beige suit buckling over his shoulder blades as he swings his briefcase to and fro. Beside him, his ex-girlfriend sees me. Laughs. Curly black hair and fat wide calves. A skirt too long for her body, it cuts her short. She turns to him and says, She is behind us. He says something back. Does not look at me.

He is angry because we fell into a tender discussion, after this long year, and it went sour. He says abortion is a Fringe Issue for this country. I said, No, not for women. Easy for you to say as a white man. Not for me. And he said, You mean you really think about the abortion issue every day? I thought. Then: I think about it a lot, yes. It's about our basic rights in this country. It is not just abortion. He said, You're just being contrary. And he swashed one hand at me. Would not look at me. He stared at the TV a while. I said, This is how I genuinely feel. I am not being contrary. We just disagree; it's not a big deal. He stared on. Would not say a word. Finally, he got up slowly, cleaned his glass in the sink, and put on his coat to go. Taking leaving slowly, I knew he was waiting for me to say something. You're leaving? I said. And he said, I think so, yeah.

I have learned to let the leavers go. Try to stop them and I am caught in something I do not want, a cycle that goes on and on and on and on and is no good for any part of me.

Okay, I said. I laughed a little. Bye, I said. He said, Bye, and walked up the stairs and out the door.

Four days later, I figured he had moved on, forgotten, decided to be friends again. It was just a political debate, I thought, nothing to end a friendship. I called him up and said, Hello, just calling to say hi, give me a ring.

He called back but said only, Jacob here, reminding you that you have lunch duty tomorrow. You get in touch with Nicole Holt if you need a sub.

And then, another week later and back at school, he has gone completely silent. I decide to let him be.

Last Day

On the last day, we wake up and have coffee together—Lexi, BP, and I. BP says he doesn't have to go to work today. That he'll hang around until I'm done with class, walk the dogs, maybe fish a little.

Great, I say.

Lexi pours him some coffee. She is still bristly about this, I can tell, but she is trying to be kind. I'm sure she'll pray for us later.

So, Lexi, says BP, are you glad to be done with the year?

So glad, she says. It's been hard to get used to this place.

Really? I say.

Yeah, she says, Oh, yeah. My last school was not a boarding school, so much simpler. Way fewer rich kids. Way easier. They just told us what to teach and we taught it.

I'd hate that, I say.

BP laughs.

We all go off to school. We pass Mr. Griffiths on our way, and he bellows hello, and Mrs. Souci, who smiles and winks at me, and the Blockhead on his bicycle, blonde tufts blowing, and Mr. O'Malley with his handlebar mustache twisted into points, and the students in their summer wear—the bright pants, the ruffled cotton skirts, the white polos.

BP comes to the Arts Building and kisses me goodbye.

Wooo! someone screams, and I turn and see Penelope. Ms. Jaaaaames, she says. She laughs, and then Steven behind her laughs, too.

Ms. James, I hear. And I turn, and it is the Headmaster, and he is standing with this arms folded.

Oh, run, says Penelope, and she and Steven rush into the building.

Yes, I say.

I took an early walk this morning, he says. He looks at BP. Says, A word in my office after class, please, he says.

Oh, I say, I don't think I'll be able to make it.

Won't be able to make it?

Right.

We need to speak again.

No, I say.

He stares at me a minute. A very, very long minute. The kids walk past us, heading for class. They holler. YAY! shouts a boy, LAST DAY!

Hey, Ms. James! screams Ruth.

I think she's in trouble, says Iris. They run into the building laughing.

You understand what this means? he says.

It means I quit, I say.

He nods his head once, very abruptly, and says, You're breaking your contract, then?

I suppose I am, I say.

Very well, he says. You won't get a recommendation from us in the future. It will be hard for you to get another teaching job around here if you quit.

Maybe. I try to keep my voice light, as if this is all easy enough for me.

I'll be in touch with our lawyers, he says.

Okay, I say.

We both stand there. He is waiting for something. His tick kicks in, shoulders pressing up. up. up. up.

You're giving up on your responsibilities, he says. You're walking away from what you committed to do. Now *I'll* have to spend the summer searching for another artist to take your place.

I shrug. Looks like it, I say.

He shakes his head. Raises one hand and shakes his finger. Says, You ought to know better. This is really irrespon–

I've had enough. I walk away. Turn my back on him and walk away.

He says to my back, It's better for the school, anyway, if you're not here. It's better for all of us.

And he walks away. And the sun is shining. And BP puts his arm around my shoulder and squeezes and says, *Hallelujiah!*, exaggerated like a preacher, and we laugh, and I go inside to say goodbye to my nine. My nine wild sweet students.

*   *   *

It is not so much these people, this place, as it is the institution. The trickle-down of power, and how they take advantage, perpetuate. The Church. With its shiny gold chalices and its silences. It is that history, enacted here, which trundles up all of my history, all of my past.

Lunch

When I go back at lunchtime, I do not hear Lexi. Andie's gone, too; so she and BP must be fishing somewhere.

I brew more coffee. I cook eggs. Breakfast for lunch. Later, there will be a last-day picnic on the big Gatsby lawn. I won't go. There's no one to say goodbye to. I'll see Mrs. Souci tonight, and Nicole and Lucy. I've said goodbye to my students. I'll see Andrew when I go down to Portland. He is leaving, too. *Exodus*, he said. And that's all.

The eggs sizzle in the frying pan. Scrambled. I take my plate and sit in the living room. The grass is green, the dogwood tree blooms white, little birds jump from the brick wall to the lawn to the branches.

I go back upstairs, and think—I remember thinking—what a strange quiet this is.

And then Mr. O'Malley calls and says, "Have you seen your roommate today? She didn't show up for class and we haven't heard from her," something in me catches. Something is not right. Like Miss Clavel, I'd raise one finger and go searching for Madeline.

No, I say. Not since breakfast. She was here for breakfast.

Can you check and see if she's there? he says.

Yes, I say, I'll call you back.

I go upstairs and knock very lightly, first, on her door. And then harder. Wait just a second. All of this in a few seconds, but it feels like time stretches on and on and on. No sound. Silence. I press my hand against the door. And then, I know, I have to open it.

I knew when I got home that something was not right. The house had the feel of no one else breathing in it, of something off.

But I thought maybe my sense was wrong. Maybe it was nothing horrific.

And it wasn't, it was not horrific. It was only that she was not there. Her bed was empty. It was made. The covers were pulled up over the pillows. The room was neat. Very, very neat. Except for a dirty pair of socks on the floor, lying crumpled side by side. That was all. And a note on the pillow, which I picked up and did not open.

I went back downstairs and called Mr. O'Malley. Stood staring out the open back door at the ditch the men had dug, now covered up with dirt, little baby blades of grass beginning to poke up.

She isn't here, I said.

Okay, he said. You don't know where she might be? Did she say anything to you this morning?

No, I said, not that I remember.

No one's seen her today, he said. No one but you.

And BP, I said.

Mr. O'Malley cleared his throat. I heard you'll be leaving us, he said. We can address that later.

I think it's all taken care of, I said. Nothing to address.

Let me know if you hear anything about Lexi.

Yes, I said.

I hung up, looked at the note in my hand. Praying it was not a suicide note. Praying she had not done anything like this. Please please please. I'm sorry for all the times that I made fun of you. I'm sorry for all the times I mocked you. I'm sorry for all the times I hated you. You're not a bad person. You're not, you're not. I am. Me and my cantankerousness. Me and my anger.

Dear Anne,
I've left the school. Please don't tell anyone until tonight. We need a head start. My parents will come after me and try to bring me home. They would never understand. I am with Jess. I am fine.
Lexi

I sit down on the couch, grateful, and I cry for this long year.

Pretty

Finally, I walk back to the kitchen to wash the dishes. Wipe my nose. Look out the window for Andie and BP.

And she walks through the front door, bag in hand, face all red. Wearing a skirt and some black flats, and a red short sleeved sweater. Dressed for freedom.

Lexi? I say. You're back?

She nods. Sets down her bag.

But why? I say. What happened?

She shrugs. I couldn't go, she said. We got to New Hampshire, and I made Jessica turn back. I couldn't go. I felt called back.

Where's Jessica?

She left, she says, and then she begins to cry. Little heaving sobs up from her shoulders.

Please don't tell anyone here, she says. Please.

I walk up the five steps. I say, But this is not the only world, Lexi, this little Catholic world. You don't have to follow these stupid rules.

You don't understand, she says: *Yes.* I do.

Ink

That afternoon, Lexi goes to the picnic, and all my things are packed. BP will come up soon to take me down to Portland. We'll stay there awhile. Maybe I'll go back to Crested Butte for the summer. Maybe forever. Maybe he'll come. I hope he'll come. We talked about it once last week, whether or not he could leave the shop. He said his friend Mike could manage it. A trial run, he said. Yes, yes, I said. But something in me knows this isn't forever. Something in me knows I'll be leaving him soon. He got me through this year, I think, and we'll have to say goodbye, too. I'm drawn back to the mountains, their wide stretch across the horizon and snowy caps in spring. He's born of this coastal place, with a business he'll never leave. We're separate, we're running opposite. I'll go, back to my friends, back home to my arid air.

I walk down to the bay with Andie, and find eight squid lying dead on the rocks, their bodies clearish white, smeared in streaks of black, the ink they shed as they were hooked and dying. They were left here on the rock, in the sun, to rot. Not to be used for bait. Not to be tossed back. No, they laid in the sun to dry out slowly. The days are hot, the nights still cold.

Their eyes are round and black and ringed in white, so they are staring up at me. Waiting. Waiting for something. As if they are saying—*why?*

I stare down at them. I hope they are still alive, that if I toss them back, they'll soak up the water again and squish away with that funny gathering-and-extending swim of theirs.

I pick up each one, sticky skin, and throw it in at the edge of the water, and watch to see. Four times, I throw. Each one bobs in the waves, tentacles dangling. Dead dead dead.

The wind blows off the water. The sun goes down. No dramatic set tonight, just a yellow glow that fades to deep blue. It is cold. I pull my sweater closer to my body. But I can't stop trying. I pick up the last four, one by one. Try not to look at their big black eyes. How they stared into the sun as they dried out. Watched the sun press into them. How it must have stung. Who did this? Who would do this? What kind of person? I am angrier and angrier, and I toss each one in and wait to see if maybe—maybe the water will do the trick. Maybe they are alive.

Once they're all back in the water, I wait. I watch until it is dark and they have bobbed away. One has washed back up, but I throw him in again. I wait until I can't see anymore, and then I turn and walk uphill. I walk home, and I imagine how they came alive offshore, how the water soaked in and soothed their eyes and soothed their squid-skin, and made them translucent again, as squid are meant to be, and they pulled in their tentacles and pushed them back out and it was almost like they were singing as they swam away. They were back where they belonged. And I could hear them as I walked up to the house. I could hear the way their squid song rose above the water.

Acknowledgements:

I'm indebted to the people who helped bring this book into the world: First, to the Braddock Avenue Books publishers and designers, Jeffrey Condran and Robert Peluso, as well as Karen Antonelli. Thank you for believing in the book, for the time and care you've put into readying it for publication, for the edits that have made it stronger, and for ushering it into others' hands. Thank you.

Sections of the book were first published in Cream City Review (Vol. 33, Issue 1) and Meridian (Issue 21). Thank you, Jay Johnson and Elaine Bartlett, editors of the respective journals, for your work with the stories and the faith you helped give me to finish the book.

I'm also grateful to the people who read drafts and offered invaluable feedback, especially Tim O'Brien, Joan Maki Bryan, Amy Brown, Lucas Stock, Krista Ferguson, and other members of the workshop. Thank you also to Deirdre McNamer, whose faith in my writing and hours (and hours) of feedback helped me find this story.

As always, tremendous thanks to friends and family who have offered writerly support, camaraderie, and love. The Mays, the Primeaus (for always believing), the Moores. Brian and Jenn Scheck-Kahn, Anna Brecke, Matthew Lansburgh, Jericho Brown, Megan Gannon, Beth O'Leary Anish, Mike Martin (especially for the introduction to BAB), Ellen Goldstein, Josie Sigler, Danielle Krcmar, Jan Johnson, Candice Smith Corby, Rebecca Loren, and Alexis Deise.

Finally, to the Millay Colony, where I shaped these pages, many thanks for the beauty of that place, the time, and the quiet to finish this book.

About the Author

Rachel May's first book, *Quilting with a Modern Slant*, was named a Best Book of 2014 by Library Journal and Amazon.com and reviewed in *The Chicago Tribune, The LA Times, The Providence Journal,* and MarthaStewartLiving.com. A collection of sewn images and prose, *The Experiments: A Legend in Pictures & Words,* is forthcoming (Dusie Press, March 2015), and her writing has been thrice nominated for the Pushcart Prize and awarded the William Allen Creative Nonfiction Award, the Geraldine McLoud Commendation, and noted in more than a dozen other contests. Her writing has appeared most recently in *Michigan Quarterly Review, Indiana Review, New Delta Review, Memoir(And),* and *Cream City Review,* and she's been awarded residencies from The Vermont Studio Center and The Millay Colony. www.rachelsmay.com

CPSIA information can be obtained
at www.ICGtesting.com
Printed in the USA
FFOW02n1608100416
23106FF